VIEW FROM THE SIDEROAD

A COLLECTION *of* UPPER PENINSULA STORIES

SHARON M. KENNEDY

Modern History Press

Ann Arbor, MI

ISBN 978-1-61599-692-6 paperback
ISBN 978-1-61599-693-3 hardcover
ISBN 978-1-61599-694-0 eBook

Published by
Modern History Press   www.ModernHistoryPress.com
Ann Arbor, MI 48105   info@ModernHistoryPress.com
Tollfree 888-761-6268   FAX 734-663-6861

Distributed by Ingram (USA/Canada), Bertram's Books (UK/EU)

Library of Congress Cataloging-in-Publication Data

Names: Kennedy, Sharon M., 1947- author.
Title: View from the sideroad : a collection of Upper Peninsula stories / Sharon M. Kennedy.
Description: Ann Arbor, MI : Modern History Press, [2022] | Summary: "A
  compilation of short stories depicting the struggles and lives of
  contemporary adults in the unforgiving rural environment of Michigan's
  Upper Peninsula"-- Provided by publisher.
Identifiers: LCCN 2022037624 (print) | LCCN 2022037625 (ebook) | ISBN
  9781615996926 (paperback) | ISBN 9781615996933 (hardcover) | ISBN
  9781615996940 (epub)
Subjects: LCSH: Upper Peninsula (Mich.)--Fiction. | LCGFT: Short stories.
Classification: LCC PS3611.E625 V54 2022 (print) | LCC PS3611.E625
  (ebook) | DDC 813/.6--dc23/eng/20220808
LC record available at https://lccn.loc.gov/2022037624
LC ebook record available at https://lccn.loc.gov/2022037625

To Kyle, Sakari, and my daughter, Stephanie, whose faith in me never waivers.

Also by Sharon M. Kennedy

The SideRoad Kids: Tales from Chippewa County

Life in a Tin Can: A Collection of Random Observations

Contents

Introduction

Although fictitious, some of the stories in *View from the SideRoad* are loosely based on tales I heard throughout my youth. My Dad was an Irishman who never missed an opportunity to embellish something his buddies had told him. Set in Goetzville, "The Premature Passing of Howdy Blanks" was one of his favorite tall-tales. Mom was also a storyteller and her rendition of Barbeau's "Vance and the Venison" was repeated every Thanksgiving. "The Upstairs Renter" was inspired by my trip to Ireland. It's about a Sault Ste. Marie man who slowly sinks into madness as he writes his novel. Gardenville's "Summer Will Not Come Again" is a story that epitomizes the love between a husband and wife and the innocence of their young granddaughter. Les Cheneaux's "Long-Suffering Edith" tells the tale of a woman who does not want another child. "Junk Drawer Blues" expresses the feelings of a gal from Shingleton who gets on the wrong freeway. When she finally arrives at her destination, the behavior of her lover is a thorough disappointment. "Aunt Betty's Secrets" takes place in Detour Village. It's a tale about relatives who search for money by rifling through their dead cousin's belongings. "Forgive Us Our Sins" is an example of how a religious fanatic from Pickford can turn his wife into a non-believer. "December's Quarry" illustrates the heartache endured by a Gulliver family when poverty grinds them down. Although the towns mentioned in the book do exist, the characters and situations are not real and do not represent any specific person, dead or alive.

Tank

Tank had sailed on the *Joseph L. Block*, a Great Lakes freighter, for more than 30 years. He was short, overweight, bald, and dirty. Especially dirty. He had this thing about water. He didn't mind sailing on it from March through the end of the season in mid-January, but the thought of standing underneath a shower or sitting in a tub made him cringe. Other than being dirty, Tank had no faults. He was a good Christian from Trenary, a tiny town in Michigan's Western Upper Peninsula famous for its Finnish cinnamon dunking toast. He didn't drink hard liquor, smoke pot, sniff cocaine, stick needles in his veins, or chase women. He had no wife or children that he knew of, no close friends, no family other than his elderly mother, and no lawyers chasing him. But Tank did have two things he treasured—his red 1999 Ford F-350 diesel truck and his mother's Pomeranian, Punk.

I met Tank in January of 2005 when we shared a room at the Holiday Inn near the Great Lakes Maritime Academy in Traverse City. The company we worked for, ArcelorMittal, owned the *Block* and had sent some of us men for two weeks of training. We were engine room wipers which means we pushed a broom or mop and didn't do much else. Once we passed this class, we'd be certified Q-MEDs. Don't ask me what that means because I didn't ask when I was told I'd become one if I was sharp enough to pass the tests. I could have cared less. I was happy pushing a broom and occasionally mopping the engine room floor, but I was pressured into this classroom business by my gal, Rita.

Anyway, I rolled into Traverse City late Sunday afternoon. I was driving my gray 2004 Chevy S-10 pickup, and I was tired. When I got to the hotel, I asked the little lady behind the desk to point me in the direction of my room. She handed me a card for 304 and told me to take the elevator and follow my nose. I've stayed at lots of motels and hotels—some dumps, some high class—but I never stayed in one that had a peculiar odor like this one. It smelled like somebody had died a long time ago, but the authorities had just found the body and decided to leave it where it was. The stench worsened as I got to my floor. When I got to my room, I was ready to pass out.

I'll tell you, I'm a big man. At 59, I'm broad across the chest, tall, strong, muscular—boxed in the ring for pay in my younger years—and I've never run from anyone or anything, but when I slipped that plastic card into the slot and that green light popped up telling me the door would open, I was ready to bolt. I can't say I took a deep breath because I was trying not to breathe at all, not wanting to inhale that odor. I turned the handle and walked in.

That's when I met Tank. He was lying on the bed closest to the window. The heat was cranked up to about 90, his boots and socks were on the floor, and he was tapping his feet to the beat of a Don Ho tune coming from a Discovery Channel special. Vomit rose to my throat, but I swallowed it down and threw my gear on the bed nearest the bathroom. Tank sat up straight and saluted. "Tank Windsor at your service," he said. "Glad to make your acquaintance." He stuck out a grubby hand. I had no choice but to shake it.

"I'm Carl," I said. "How're you doing?"

"Doin' good. Got no troubles as long as I got Punk to keep me out of 'em. How about you?" Tank was still holding my hand, actually squeezing it, and I had to wiggle my fingers from his grasp. Punk was the size of a minute, but he growled like he was an Irish wolfhound.

"I'm fine. Drove in from Illinois. Little town called Odin about an hour's drive north of St. Louis. Where you from?" My head was spinning from the heat and the stench, but I tried to act normal. Tank's coveralls were filthy. A crawling, bushy black beard covered every inch of his face except his forehead and eyes. His black eyebrows covered them. His hands were cracked and calloused and unusually white for a man who obviously never showered. Maybe he had a medical condition.

"Me? I'm from everywhere and nowhere. Been sailin' so long, I ain't had time to settle in one place since I left Trenary the summer of 1965. When the boat lays up in January, me and Punk hop in the truck and follow the road. It don't matter where we go. We got nobody to please or answer to, so we please ourselves and answer to no one. You got a wife?"

"No, not now. Had four throughout the years, but none now. Got a girlfriend in Brimley, though. Excuse me a minute," I said and headed for the toilet. I couldn't keep my lunch down.

"You all right in there?" Tank hollered. "You eat somethin' that didn't agree with you? You want some Pepto? I got some tablets in my pocket."

"I'm okay. I'll be right out," I yelled.

"You don't look too good, old boy," Tank said when I sat on my bed. "Can I get you anythin'?" He looked sincere, but I knew I couldn't stay in this room.

"I'll be okay. Just let me catch my breath and get some fresh air."

"It too hot in here for you? I can turn the heat down. There, is that better?"

"That's fine. Thanks." I was trying to breathe without inhaling.

"You got medical troubles?" he asked.

"Not that I know of."

"Well, then, it's just a case of nerves. This your first time here?"

"Yeah. Yours?"

"No, third time. I think I know the answers, but when I take the test they fly away as fast as ducks fly from a shotgun."

"Don't they say third time's a charm?"

"How many times you say you been married?"

"You got me there."

Tank scratched his armpit, increasing the stench. "Some fellows like to talk," he said. "Others don't. Take me, for instance. I don't say much most of the time unless I'm with Punk. No dogs allowed in this fancy joint, so this little beggar has to stay in the truck. I snuck him in underneath my jacket, but I know he can't spend the night. I'll leave the truck runnin' so he don't freeze to death. I'll bet Punk's got me trained better than any wife you ever had. I'll take him for a walk now before it gets too dark." He put on his socks and boots and grabbed his Carhartt jacket from where he had thrown it across a chair.

As soon as the door closed, I slid the window open and called the front desk. "Get me another room," I shouted to the little lady. "I'm in 304 and if I stay here much longer, I'll be dead." She said she'd try her best but in the meantime she suggested I calm down. Easy for her to say. I dug in my suitcase for a bottle of Mesmerize cologne and sprayed a good amount of it throughout the room. Then I figured I might as well hang up some of my shirts so they wouldn't wrinkle. I'm fussy that way. Whether I'm in this room for five minutes or five hours, I don't want wrinkled shirts. When I opened the closet, it was empty. Either Tank hadn't unpacked or he didn't have anything other than the clothes on his back. I didn't see a suitcase, backpack, duffle bag, or even a plastic bag from K-Mart. Except for the lingering smell and the indentation on the bedspread, there was no indication Tank had ever been in this room.

Maybe he was a bum who had wandered in from the cold and found a door unlocked. Yeah, that must be it. I didn't think I'd be seeing him again. When I looked out the window, his truck was gone. Good. I thumbed through the phone book, found a Pizza Hut, ordered a twelve incher with the works and a Diet Pepsi, and clicked on Fox News. I stretched out on the bed and called my woman. She answered on the second ring like she always does because I trained her. It sure is great knowing there's a gal waiting for me who doesn't ask questions. I trained her on that count, too. If you train them right from the get-go, it makes life a whole lot easier.

It wasn't long before my pizza arrived. I ate my fill, switched channels until I found "City Confidential" and settled down for the night. I must have dozed off because it seemed like my head had just hit the pillow when someone was shaking me awake. For a few minutes, I couldn't remember where I was until Tank's bushy face was next to mine.

"Mornin' Sleepin' Beauty. Time to rise and whine," he said. "I'm gonna walk Punk now. Class starts in an hour." As he was going out the door he turned and said, "Say, what's that awful stink? Hit me full force when I walked in here last night. The place smelled like a whore house."

With a wave of his hand, he was gone, or maybe I should say his body was gone. I thought I was going to hurl again, but everything stayed down. I opened the window, turned off the heat, and sprayed more cologne. The tub was dry as I stepped in it and there was no sign of a wet towel. Why should that surprise me? After a quick shower, I dressed in my new beige Remington shirt and khaki cargo pants, slicked my hair into place, combed my eyebrows, plucked some wayward nose hairs, and put on my rings. I swung my arms through my new leather jacket and pulled on my Columbia boots. I was ready to face that little lady at the front desk and demand a room change. I couldn't believe I had slept through the night as well as the stench, but I knew I'd never make it through another one.

When I got to the front desk, I was in for a surprise. The little lady was gone and in her place was a feisty-looking matron who informed me no other rooms were available. One look at the old gal and the fight went out of me. I could tell she wasn't moved by my charm or good looks. I wandered over to the breakfast buffet and fixed myself some instant oatmeal, two English muffins with peanut butter, poured a cup of black coffee, and sat at one of the tables. The coffee was just right. Not too strong. Not too bitter. The food was putting me in a good mood, so I called my gal and she answered on that second ring. Rita wished me luck. I hadn't set foot in a classroom in over 45 years and then it was only the eighth grade. I knew I was going to need all the luck I could get.

I drank the last of my coffee and returned to the room. I brushed my teeth and gargled with some fancy California mouthwash called TheraBreath, a gift from Rita. Most of the time, she's a good old gal, but she has a wicked temper. I called her again just to make sure she was home and not running around with some other fellow. I reassured her she was my main squeeze which may or may not have been the truth. I learned a long time ago you got to keep the gals guessing so they treat you right and not take advantage. I closed my briefcase, put on my gloves and left the room. It was only a short walk to the classroom, but the wind blew cold off Lake Michigan and sliced right through me.

"Over here, Craig. I saved you a seat." I walked into the empty room and took the chair Tank pointed to. "It's nice to get here early," he said. "We got the best spots." He had plunked us in the back row, as far from the whiteboard as possible. I've only got one good eye and wondered how I was going to see anything.

"Name's Carl," I corrected, but it made no difference.

As the room filled with men, only latecomers sat by us. I was worried they might think I was the smelly one, but anybody could tell just by looking at Tank that he hadn't seen a bar of soap in years. The teacher, a man who looked weather-worn and stern, walked to the front of the room and told us the next two weeks might be rough sailing, but we'd make it through if we paid attention which is what I did.

The time went fast and as the week wound down, I was more relaxed and sure of myself. The class was interesting. I learned about ballast and gauges, what to do in emergencies including a pirate attack, and a dozen other things I might remember if I don't forget them. When Friday's session was over, I headed for my room and Tank headed for his truck and Punk. On Saturday he disappeared early, and I had the room to myself.

I looked at a note of encouragement from my gal and that got me thinking about all the women I've known. The good ones, bad ones, mean ones, religious ones, the sober and the drunk ones. Then I thought about Ma. She passed away five years ago. She always loved me no matter what I did, and I did a lot of stuff I'm not proud of. What got me thinking about her was Tank. He talks in his sleep. Every night he yells, "Ma, it'll be okay." He mumbles for a long time before he cries. I never heard a grown man cry before. In the morning, he always asks if I heard him blubbering. I say yeah. This morning he told me about his mother.

"She's in a nursin' home," he said. "Not on welfare, though. I pay the bills. Her memory's gone, and she don't know who I am. Punk's her dog, but they don't allow dogs at the home, so I promised her I'd take good care of him. When I sail, I put Punk in a kennel, and it just about kills me. He's an old dog and probably won't last much longer." When he left the room, I cracked the window and sprayed more cologne.

The weekend went fast. I called Rita every couple hours, but I didn't mention the class or anything else. I made her do all the talking. I learned a long time ago to say as little as possible so my tongue doesn't slip up and get me in hot water with the women. That's why I love cell phones. I can be with Charlotte and tell Rita I'm in my bunk watching the news while I'm really getting it on with Charlotte. Well, anyway, Tank returned late Sunday night. He greeted me like we were old buddies who hadn't seen each other in years. He smelled worse than ever. Monday evening, he didn't show up after his walk with Punk. For the rest of the week, I roomed alone. It didn't take long for the smell of him to disappear or maybe I had just gotten used to it. I asked the guys if they knew where he was, but nobody did.

By Friday, the temp had dropped to negative 20, the course was over, and I was ready to head north on I-75 with my certificate as a bona fide Q-MED in my briefcase. I couldn't wait to show it to Rita. I left early Saturday morning and called her as I was crossing the Mackinac Bridge. As usual, she answered on that second ring, but her voice sounded different. She said a friend of mine had stopped by with a letter addressed to me. She said the fellow had a strong smell about him, but he was pleasant in a sad sort of way. Then she asked if I wanted her to read the letter. I said go ahead.

Rita read, "Just a note to let you know I got word Ma died Monday. I was goin' pass the test this time and be a Q-MED, but I was so broke up, I had to leave and take care of things. I also decided to retire. Got a nice nest egg saved. Just wanted to let you know you were real good company except for that awful stuff you sprayed. Here's my number. Keep in touch. Be seein' you, Tank."

I asked Rita how Tank knew her. She said she had called the room one evening, but I wasn't in. Tank answered the phone and they visited for an hour. She said she called a dozen more times, but each time I was out and wasn't answering my cell. Eventually, Tank asked for her address. Her next words nearly knocked me off my seat.

"Don't bother coming around again," she said. "I've decided to try my luck with someone else. You might as well turn your truck around and head back to Illinois. It's been fun, Carl, but it's over." She hung up. When I called back, it went to the answering machine. I called and called, but not once did she pick up the phone. Finally, I called Tank.

"Heard you dropped by Rita's place," I said and before I could say anything more, he informed me they were a couple. "I took one look at your little lady and I was hooked. After I left that note for you, I went straight to the *Ojibway*, Sault Ste. Marie's most expensive hotel, got me a room, and soaked in the tub for an hour. Then I went to the barber shop once owned by Wimpy Smith and got a shave and my eyebrows trimmed. Then I bought a mountain of clothes at JC Penneys, and after that, I traded in my truck for a snazzy new black Corvette. Then I called Rita and asked if she was busy. She answered on the second ring like you said she always does. We went to dinner at the Robin's Nest and talked for hours. The upshot is I asked her to marry me, and she said yes. We're drivin' to Vegas tomorrow to escape the cold, and Punk can hardly wait. All's fair in love and war, right Craig? We'll be wed in the Elvis Chapel. No hard feelin's, right?"

"Right," I said and hung up the cell. I tore my Q-MED certificate into tiny pieces and threw it out the window. I won't need it if I'm giving up sailing. I was only doing it because Rita pushed me. Women. You can't trust them, not for a minute. And I should know. I've had hundreds. I got off the freeway at the Clare exit and headed south. Then I called an ex-wife. She answered on that second ring, just like I knew she would because I trained her. Life is good when you know how to play it.

Zelly's Midnight Battle

"Damn you cats. Quit waking me up at midnight. If you don't shut up, I'll shoot the lot of you which, of course, will bring Constable Miller of Dafter pounding on my front door in the morning." With that, Zelly reaches for the shotgun propped by the side of her bed, walks downstairs, opens the back door of her well-kept house, and shoots into the night sky. The shrieking stops as she hears strays, as well as her own cats, run in every direction. She shouts a loud *scat* into the air and fires again. On the way back to her bedroom, she misses the top step. It isn't until she hits the floor that she realizes her mistake.

"Goddamnit," she says as she props herself into an upright position. "Goddamn everything to hell and back especially the cats, the steps, and my useless old legs." She climbs back into bed, but sleep has left her. She tosses and turns. The Westclox on her nightstand reads just past twelve. Every summer night it's the same routine. The neighboring cats fight hers. Try as she might, she can't convince her three toms to stay in the house where they belong. They insist on sleeping on her good davenport during the day and spending the night prowling the neighborhood. Just yesterday, Barney, the oldest, came home with an entry wound in his left leg and an exit wound in his right eye. There's always something stealing her peace. If it isn't screaming cats at midnight, it's a wounded one in the morning. If it isn't a squirrel jumping from the spruce tree to her metal roof, it's a rat running through the rafters. Zelly lies in bed and worries about everything under the sun until the sun comes up and she falls back to sleep just about the time it's time to get up and get going.

She rearranges herself, pulls the covers underneath her chin, and thinks about her life. It isn't a bad one. God saw fit to spare her the torment of a husband and children. At an early age, she had her fill of cooking and cleaning and caring for her younger sister, Rene. When she was nine, Zelly was put out to labor as a char and decided she wanted no part of domestic life if all it involved was drudgery. She scrimped and saved until she had enough money to buy an old Royal typewriter. Then she taught herself to type. At 15, she got an office job.

She worked for Beyer Cement in Calumet until five years ago when she turned 65, her boss told her it was time to retire, and she moved back to Dafter. She knows she has plenty of good years left in her, but she has no idea how to use all the time on her hands.

But tonight it isn't just the cats keeping Zelly awake. It's worrying about her sister who stopped by yesterday with some disturbing news. Rene wants to leave her husband and asked Zelly if she could move in with her. Zelly's first response was astonishment followed by outrage, but she couldn't show her true feelings to her sibling. She's caught in the middle of an awful mess. If she refuses Rene's request, there'll be hell to pay. If she gives in, she might as well check herself into a mental institution because Rene will drive her crazy. She was always the floozy of the family, and Zelly knows Rene will put a red light in the window as sure as day follows night.

"If I had a husband, things would be different," Zelly muses aloud. "Rene wouldn't dream of asking to move in with me. Just because I'm a spinster she thinks I don't have a real life, but what the hell do you call what I'm doing if it isn't living? I breathe like everybody else. I have feelings like the rest of the family, and I don't want to be bothered with a middle-aged strumpet. Hell, I'm wide awake now. I might as well get up and make a cup of tea."

Zelly putters in her kitchen. "Why the hell does the family always take advantage of me?" she asks the tea kettle. "And why didn't I tell Rene the truth that I don't want her here and the spare room belongs to the cats? Why am I such a coward? Why do I get everything backwards?" Zelly's verbal monologue continues until the kettle whistles. She opens the tea canister and scoops out some loose leaves. She tosses them in a fancy teapot and puts it on a wooden tray next to her favorite china cup and saucer. She fills a matching serving plate with sugar cookies she baked two days ago. She carries everything to the living room and chooses the only thing of value her father left her—an ancient leather chair, soft and well-worn from years of holding his drunken body.

She has a habit of sitting in that chair, drinking tea, and surveying her comfortable room. Sometimes she sits for hours, in a stupor as she refers to her condition, and looks around the room at the pictures on the walls, the furniture, the books, the plants, and the carpet. In other words, she surveys the objects that complete her life. It's as if she's glued to her chair. This condition has not come upon her recently but has been with her from childhood. As the older of two children, Zelly has lived most of her life in a dream state. On the family farm, there was always endless work and never enough money. Death was a constant companion and sorrow the natural state of being. Zelly survived by carving a pleasant world of daydreams. *Don't look back, don't look back* was her mantra and the impetus pushing her forward from an early age.

The clock on the mahogany buffet strikes 1:30 a.m. She finishes her tea, puts the dishes in the sink, and climbs the stairs to her bedroom. This time she doesn't forget the top step. Maybe she can get a little more sleep before the July sun announces the dawn of another day. She closes the door and switches off the light. Before reaching the comfort of her mattress, she stubs her toe on the wheel of the antique iron bed that once belonged to her mother and in which Zelly was conceived.

"Goddamn you goddamned wheel," she says and pulls the pink sheet up to her chin. In the distance she hears the shriek of cats as the toms fight over the females. She sticks her arm out from underneath the sheet and reaches for the flask of Jack Daniels in the nightstand's top drawer. After a good slug, she rolls towards the wall, oblivious to everything except her own rhythmic breathing. Sleep will soon come and another night will soon pass and all will soon be well if she can just muster the courage to shoot the goddamned cats and tell Rene to go to hell and stay there.

Vance and the Venison

Stud Strong of Barbeau was tracking a wounded deer on a brisk November morning when he saw smoke coming from a shack that stood north of the creek on his property. He wanted to check who was there, but first he had to follow the buck's bloody trail into the forest. When the animal finally collapsed, Stud took off his gloves and slit its throat with his hunting knife. Then he gutted it. The heat from the spikehorn's innards warmed his hands, and as the blood made contact with the cold air, it congealed underneath his fingernails.

Stud was a strong man. He had no trouble hoisting the young buck onto his back. There wasn't much snow to plow through and now that its innards were gone, the buck's weight was manageable. Stud made his way to the clearing where the shack stood. He dropped his load and kicked the door open just as a stranger decided to open it. The force of Stud's foot caught the man off guard and down he went, making more noise than a flock of Canadian geese heading south. He curled his arms around his belly and drew up his legs. He was dressed in black and looked like a black woolen ball. Stud dropped to one knee and offered a hand. The man didn't seem to notice. He was too busy nursing his hurt gut. There was nothing to do now except wait for the fellow to come around.

As Stud's eyes adjusted to the dim light, he glanced around the shack. From the looks of the place, he figured someone had been living on his property for quite a while. There was a pile of hardwood stacked in one corner, an Army blanket on the cot, and a coffee pot beginning to boil over on the woodstove. The place was warm and dry and inviting. He recognized a ratty old handmade rag rug in front of the stove as well as a piece of torn oilcloth that served as a covering for the makeshift table. Last April, when Mavis, his wife, did her spring cleaning, she had ordered Stud to throw these things in the ravine behind their barn. He also saw chipped cups and plates he recognized as his own. And lodged in a chopping block in the middle of the room was his favorite broadax, the one he thought his brother-in-law, Toad, had nicked. The shack was small and the fire was hot. Stud took a cup from the shelf above the stove and poured himself some coffee. Then he removed his plaid woolen jacket and hung it over the back of the kitchen chair. He put his cap on the table. As snow melted from his boots, it left a little puddle beneath his feet. He reached for a rag hanging on a nail and wiped the water. Then he threw the rag at the stranger's head.

"Time go get up, old boy," he said. He stirred sugar into his cup, leaned back in his chair, and drank the coffee as he watched the ball on the floor unwind. The first thing he saw was a rugged-looking face with deep wrinkles across his forehead. The man's eyes were a watery blue and his bushy eyebrows were the same gray as his mustache and beard. His nose dominated his face. He shook his head.

"Where am I?" he asked. His eyes looked every bit as wild as the buck's had just before the bullet hit him.

"You're in my shack," Stud said. "You're on Strong land and it looks like you've been here quite a while. Who are you?"

The stranger gripped the table's edge and heaved himself up. He wasn't thin nor was he fat, but he was strong. Stud could tell by the grip of his hand as he offered help. He reached for another cup and filled it with coffee. The man took it and sipped the scalding stuff. Then he reached for a pint of Jim Beam stored underneath the cot's mattress. He splashed some in Stud's cup and poured some in his own.

"Vance Livers Wells, at your service," he said, and made a sweeping motion with his cap as if he were addressing royalty. "Pleased to make your acquaintance." He put the cap back on his head and sat facing Stud. "And who, sir, might you be?" His eyes told Stud he already knew the answer, but he played along. He was beginning to find the character amusing.

"I'm your landlord, Stud Strong," he said. "I'm here to collect the rent." Vance offered another taste of Mr. Beam and Stud accepted. "That's one day's payment," he said. "But it looks like you're at least a year in arrears. What's your story?"

Vance took his time replying. He roused himself and threw more logs in the stove. Then he stirred a pot of stew he had cooking on the back burner. Stud wondered if the carrots, turnips, potatoes, and cabbage from his garden were adding to the flavor. Vance reached in a drawer and took out a paring knife. Then he picked up a piece of cedar and began whittling.

"Well?" Stud asked. "Just give it to me straight. What's your story? I got a buck outside that needs attention. I haven't got all day."

"You ever hear of a thing called a 'Sputnik'?" Vance asked.

"Everybody's heard of the Sputnik. What's that got to do with you nesting on my land?"

Vance whittled fast and the cedar began to take shape. "Well, it's like this. I was on my way to Canada when I took sick. I found this shack and lucky for me or I'd be just as dead as your deer. I pushed open the door and the place seemed happy to see me. I fell on the cot and slept for three days. When I finally woke up, the sun was streaming through the window and the red leaves on that big oak were falling on the porch. While I'd been sick, I dreamed of that Sputnik. I knew the Russians were up to no good, so I decided to stay put. I figured it was Providence that had led me to your shack. That's what it was. Pure Providence, so I knew I'd found me a home."

"You got any kin?" Stud asked.

"Not a soul in the world."

"The law looking for you?"

"Sure as that deer you shot, the law ain't after me." Vance finished whittling. He handed Stud his handiwork.

"What's this supposed to be?" he asked.

"Why, it's that Russian Sputnik. I've whittled hundreds of 'em and left 'em wherever I traveled, but this is the first one I ever hand-delivered."

"What am I supposed to do with it?"

"Well, that's up to you. I figure it ought to be good for a month's rent on this place."

"How do you figure that? It's my cedar you whittled with my wife's paring knife while you're sitting on her chair drinking coffee from her cup and resting your elbows on her table. So how do you figure this is worth a month's rent?"

"You're right," Vance said. "Let's call it payment for the winter."

"I could have you arrested for trespassing and theft."

"Yup, you sure could. You'd be doing me a favor. Just thinking about taking it easy for the winter, not fighting the wind and snow and setting traps to catch my supper sounds pretty good. Let's eat. Then go home and call the sheriff."

Stud did call the sheriff, but not until the first day of spring to report a neighbor had shot Duke, his best hunting dog. As for Vance, his cooking was so tasty, Stud's good nature overruled any idea of eviction. He told Vance he could stay as long as he wanted. He even stopped by twice a week with a bag of groceries and a pint of whiskey they drank over hands of poker. Stud would never admit it, but Mavis roasted a poor venison compared to Vance's. Stud and Vance became buddies. That summer Vance helped with the haying and was often invited to the big house for supper. Unfortunately, towards the end of August Stud unexpectedly died. Mavis lost no time driving the tractor to Vance's shack and telling him the sad news. Once Stud was safely in the ground, Vance took over the farm. That November he shot the biggest buck anyone had ever seen on Strong land. No spikehorn for him.

Come November, Mavis married Vance Livers Wells, and he moved into Stud's house. There was some speculation about Stud being poisoned. All spring and long into the summer he had suffered from a disease old Doc Lippit couldn't find a cure for. Mavis wasn't the easiest woman to live with. The fights between her and Stud were legendary throughout Chippewa County. People loved to gossip, but talk soon died down when everyone in the surrounding area was invited to a Thanksgiving venison feast prepared by Vance. As long as he kept Mavis out of the kitchen, folks figured his life would be a long and happy one. The newlyweds were wished well as they polished off the beautiful buck Stud Strong was never able to bring down. When the meal was over, everyone raised a glass in memory of Stud, the poorest shot in the whole of Michigan, but the nicest guy who ever drew breath.

The Frying Pan Incident

Shirley didn't mean to hurt Mother. It was an accident, pure and simple, just as most accidents usually are. It was one of those bizarre things that happen every now and then, and there's no way to explain or excuse it. When Shirley told me the story, her words tumbled out helter-skelter. She said she loved Mother and had no idea why Mother had tried to hurt her. But something happened that snowy morning of February 2, 1985 in Newberry, a nondescript town in Michigan's Upper Peninsula.

Maybe the wind caused the problem. It had howled all night and kept Shirley awake. Maybe the snow was to blame. A foot of it had fallen burying everything beneath a heavy, white shroud, forcing her to cancel her breakfast plans with a gentleman friend. She rarely socialized and the unexpected blizzard had cancelled her monthly outing, thus making her more irritable than usual. Maybe Mother was just in the wrong place at the right time. It was simply one of those sad, tragic affairs that nobody sees coming.

My name is Sis Tones. I'm a hairdresser for most of the funeral parlors in Luce County. I was widowed 31 years ago and left with two small children, a mountain of debt, and no means of support. At my husband's wake, I was appalled and dismayed at the way Barney's hair looked. It was dirty and uncombed, and his long, shaggy brown bangs hung over his eyes. I had to fight the urge to push them aside. Had he known, he would have been horrified at his appearance and leapt out of the coffin for Barney was meticulous about his grooming. As I observed his pathetically disheveled hair and bushy eyebrows, the idea entered my head to become a hairdresser. Looking at the mourners, I noticed—even in my grief—that the corpse wasn't the only one who needed a decent haircut. In an instant, I decided what to do with the rest of my life to earn a living for the kids and me. I would become a hairdresser.

That afternoon, when Barney was safely in his grave, Mr. Kelsey, the undertaker, offered to drive me home. I asked him to stop by the hairdressing school on State Street. I enrolled in Stylathon that very day. Let me tell you, it was no small task, attending school, running a house, caring for my boy and girl, making ends meet any way I could, but I was determined to succeed, and I did it all on my own. I'm a proud, independent woman.

I was working for Kelsey, Kelsey, and Kelsey when Mother was brought in. Only Shirley attended the wake and Kelsey tradition dictated that when mourners were scarce, employees filled the gap. That's how I met Shirley. We always felt the meeting was predestined. Although she was no blood relation to Mother, she chose to call her by that honored name. At 56, Shirley was an orphan. Her father had died years ago in a house fire while Shirley was dancing at the local drinking establishment. She carried a sense of guilt for the unfortunate accident. She hadn't meant to leave her cigarette burning so close to the lacy curtains, nor had she meant to administer so many sleeping pills to Daddy. Shirley had no education and possessed no skills other than the homemaking ones she taught herself at age eight when her mother ran off with the traveling Watkins man and was never heard from again.

As Mother's caregiver, her children were happy with Shirley, for she gave them the freedom they desired to ignore their mother and continue their lives without feeling one speck of guilt. Mother had been somewhat of a tyrant, and her offspring found it difficult to feel an ounce of affection for her. This arrangement suited all parties. Mother was unaware she had birthed two selfish, greedy children and, therefore, did not miss them. The children were not bothered by the schizophrenic lifestyle of their parent, and Shirley enjoyed the pretense of being lady of the manor. As she wept, she described the circumstances that led to today's wake:

Shirley had awakened early two days ago. She was cold. Her small bedroom was too far from the furnace to receive any heat, and she was not allowed to keep a heater in her room for fear it might tip over during the night and burn down the house. Although she snuggled between thick flannel sheets and various blankets, she felt no warmth. Her bed was beneath the north window and her head would have frozen had it not been for her nightcap. She went to bed cold and awoke the same or so she said.

Due to the blizzard, she was colder than usual. The wind must have been from the southeast, she reasoned, for it swept through the house as if the structure had no walls. The furnace could run all day, but it would only take the first chill from the rooms. It would not warm them. Mother had flung open the door to Shirley's bedroom and was standing at the foot of her bed, looking rather like Marley's ghost. Shirley's heart hammered from the surprise awaking. She feared the place was on fire, but could neither see nor smell smoke. Mother gripped the bedpost and shook it.

"Git up," she yelled. "Git up, you lazy thing. The cows need milking." Having said thus, Mother slammed the door and retreated. Shirley heard the creak of the chair as Mother made herself comfortable. Then the boom of Valerie Pringle's voice filled her room when Mother turned the television to the Canadian station. She outyelled the newscaster as the latter droned on and on about the blizzard conditions and warned her audience to stay home.

"Where the hell is Ma?" Mother shouted. "And where's my breakfast?"

Shirley resisted the urge to scream that "Ma" was in the Riverside graveyard in Sault Ste. Marie, had been there for well over 60 years and in all probability wasn't coming back. But, instead, she pushed aside the covers and got out of bed. The floor was icy cold. Her feet found her slippers, and she wrapped herself into her new purple velvet robe, an extravagance she had purchased at the K-Mart after-Christmas sale. She reached for her spectacles on the nightstand next to Maeve Binchy's *The Copper Beech*, Shirley had finished reading last night. When she opened her bedroom door, Mother threw a fit. "I need food," she hollered. "Where's my food? I haven't eaten in a week." As she shook her fist at Shirley, something fluttered to the floor. Shirley walked to Mother's chair and picked up a tiny blue feather. Mother's right hand was firmly closed.

"What's in your hand?" Shirley asked. Stepping closer to see what Mother held, she pried her fingers open. The blue parakeet fell on her lap. "You killed Happy," Shirley said. She picked up the little bird. His head hung limply to one side. "You killed my bird," Shirley repeated, to which Mother merely waved her hand and said, "Oh, go to hell," as she turned her attention back to the television, found the remote, and began switching channels.

Shirley wrapped Happy in tinfoil, and deposited him in a Red Owl grocery bag lining the green wastebasket. She brushed a tear from her eye. Happy was six years old and had been her friend. He would be missed. Shirley brushed more tears as they ran down her cheeks. She busied herself in the kitchen. She would mourn Happy later, but now she had to get to work. She poured water and coffee grounds into the coffee pot and turned on the burner. She felt it was too early to fry eggs and sausages, Mother's favorite food, so she took two slices of raisin bread from the freezer and put them in the toaster.

It wasn't long before the coffee was ready. Shirley caught it just before it boiled over on the burner. She removed it from the heat and pressed the lever on the toaster. Mother appeared to be dozing. No matter. Shirley would enjoy the hot coffee and toast and feed Mother later. It was much too early for either of them to be up. Mother rarely got out of her recliner before eleven o'clock. It was only quarter to seven, and the night had not yet surrendered to the day.

Shirley took the cast iron frying pan from the lower kitchen cupboard. She placed it on the stove where it would be ready when summoned to fry Mother's eggs and sausages, then she carried her coffee and toast to the living room. She balanced both on her lap while Valerie interviewed the ice dancing pair of Bourne and Kraatz who were favored to win the Canadian championships in Montreal later in the week. Both Mother and Shirley enjoyed watching the skaters. They were graceful and seemed to fly across the ice. Shirley glanced at Mother, but she appeared to be resting quietly. Shirley reached for the remote and lowered the volume which, of course, awoke Mother.

"Don't touch that channel," she yelled. "And turn the damn thing up so I can hear it. Where's my breakfast. I'm hungry. Where's Ma?"

Shirley felt her back stiffen and her heartbeats quicken as she left her chair. This was going to be another impossible day, and she felt she couldn't endure Mother one more minute. In her frustration, she splashed hot coffee on her new robe. This only added to her anger and resentment. She wasn't paid enough to endure the craziness of her life, but with no education and no marketable skills, she had no choice. "How about a nice piece of raisin toast and a cup of coffee? That'll be all right for now, won't it Mother?"

"Coffee? What's the occasion? We only have coffee at Easter and Christmas and when someone dies. Who died? Well, are you going to tell me who died? One of the in-laws? Or is it Easter or Christmas?" Her body jerked forward as she vacated her recliner. She hobbled to the kitchen table. Mother weighed less than 80 pounds but possessed such a powerful mouth her slight weight often went unnoticed. Shirley felt her entire body tensing as Mother's barrage of words cascaded around her.

"Mother, no one died and it isn't a holiday. We have coffee every morning," Shirley explained. Then she filled Mother's favorite cup with the steaming brew and stirred in a tablespoon of sugar and two teaspoons of Creamora.

"I'll hit you if you don't tell me what day it is," Mother threatened as she reached for the cup. "I'll pinch you if you lie to me. Who died? Where am I? Where's the cookies?"

Shirley was used to Mother's ways, but being used to them didn't make them any easier to accept. She found four Fig Newtons in the cookie jar, cut them into small pieces, and put them on a plate she set before Mother who placed a piece on her spoon and dunked it into the coffee. The raisin toast was burning and set off the smoke alarm. Mother ignored it, but Shirley got out the stepladder and shut the alarm off.

"Got anything to eat?" Mother asked. "I haven't eaten in a week. Got any eggs? Get to the barn and look for some, you useless thing." Mother finished her cookies. Shirley reached for the frying pan to start frying the sausages. The pan was old and heavy with carbon build-up. The interior was smooth as the most expensive Teflon coated T-Fal pan Shirley saw advertised when she was allowed to watch QVC. She placed four link sausages in the pan, along with some Irish-style fried potatoes. When they were well on their way to being ready, she cracked in two eggs. The pan was so hot, the eggs quickly crisped around the edges just the way Mother liked them.

"Since when does it take all day to fry an egg?" Mother yelled. "Did you have to go to the chicken coop? Did you have to catch the chicken and coax her into laying? Why didn't you gather the eggs yesterday? Why are you so stupid?"

The hair on Shirley's neck bristled. "It's almost ready, Mother," she said, and in an effort to relieve the tension she felt mounting between her shoulders, Shirley kicked the cabinet door beneath the sink so hard her foot went through it. She winced with pain.

"What was that noise? Somebody breaking in? Get the shotgun."

"I dropped something, Mother," Shirley lied.

"Bullshit. Somebody's here. Get the gun. Call the sheriff."

Shirley ignored Mother's orders and emptied her breakfast onto a large plate she had warmed in the oven. She cut the raisin toast in half and made a little pool of Heinz Ketchup in the middle of the plate. Mother loved ketchup. Shirley then sprinkled freshly ground pepper over the eggs.

"Here you go," she said. She forced a pleasant tone in her voice as she placed the plate before Mother. "Everything's hot, so don't burn your mouth," Shirley cautioned. "I'll get more coffee."

"There's enough food here for an army," Mother said. "There's enough food to last three, maybe four days. Here, you eat some." Mother took her butter knife and parted the food into two sections.

"No, that's for you," Shirley explained. "Eat as much or as little as you want."

"Crazy, that's what you are. Crazy, expecting an old woman to eat this much food. What'd think I'm going to do today—hitch up the team and plow a field?"

Shirley listened to Mother drone on about all the food on her plate. She listened until Mother had eaten every morsel and asked for another cookie. "I haven't eaten in a week," she said as Shirley handed Mother more Fig Newtons cut into pieces. "Are you trying to starve me?"

Thus began the daily routine of pleasing Mother. Shirley was paid $800 a month. She worked seven days a week with no respite. When she went to the supermarket, she locked Mother in the house so she wouldn't escape and get hit by a car or worse yet, get buried in a snowdrift during the winter or drown in the river during the summer. Shirley kept the house neat and tidy. She did the best she could to make Mother happy, but Mother could be difficult. It took a great deal of patience and steady nerves to shoulder the burden of being sole caregiver. Shirley listened to Mother recite a poem she had learned as a child. Over and over, every day for as long as she had been with her, Shirley listened to the words until she knew them by heart. By noon, the poem had been repeated multiple times with no end in sight. After Mother finished her breakfast, the repetition began.

"Have you heard 'My Shadow'?" Mother yelled from her chair and began repeating it until Shirley went to the back porch and screamed until she injured her throat. Her head began spinning as if she were in a crazy Tilt-a-Whirl carnival ride. She clutched the porch railing as a cold wind blew over her. She didn't know how she would survive the day. At this point in her story, the phone in Mr. Kelsey's office rang, interrupting Shirley's soliloquy. I told her I'd be right back and left her gazing at Mother in her coffin.

Shirley was clever and grateful the phone had rung. She realized she had said quite enough to Sis who was Newberry's greatest gossip. What happened next was repeated only in Shirley's mind. She had temporarily gone mad when Mother began quoting "My Shadow."

After screaming as loudly as she could, she returned to the kitchen and began washing and drying the breakfast dishes. She carefully wiped the cast iron skillet and rubbed it with Canola oil before putting it back with the other pots and pans when something inside her went haywire. Mother called out if she wanted to hear a poem. Shirley said no, but Mother wouldn't stop.

"I have a little shadow that goes in and out with me, and what can be the use of her is more than I can see. She is very, very like me from my heels up to my head..." That's when Shirley's nerves snapped. She raised the frying pan as a gesture of defiance and somehow it connected with Mother's right temple. It took one blow to silence her. She stopped reciting and gave Shirley a little smile. Then she slumped forward in her chair and was gone.

Shirley's rage immediately left her. She remained calm as she went about her morning chores. She put the pan back on the stove, ran a dishrag over the kitchen table, swept the floor, cleaned Happy's cage, and put all his food in a lunch bag. Later she would fill the outside birdfeeders. Then she made her bed and dressed in her finest black slacks and white turtleneck sweater. She went to the bathroom, washed her face, combed her hair, and applied makeup. She admired herself in the mirror. She looked serene and composed and absolutely beautiful.

She returned to the kitchen and poured coffee into a priceless Bavarian china cup she was never allowed to touch. She threw a towel over Mother's head and sat on a lovely velvet chair in the living room and considered her options. She knew nobody would miss Mother until May when the son and daughter would call and wish her a Happy Mother's Day. She knew she was safe until then. Or she could call the sheriff and tell him the truth. She could call Mr. Kelsey, her gentleman friend, and say Mother had drifted away during the night. She could call the son and daughter and explain Mother had suffered a heart attack and was now in heaven. She could call a neighbor. Or she could relax and enjoy the rest of the winter. Mother's paycheck would arrive on the third of the month as usual, and Shirley's check would arrive on the first of the month. She needn't worry about fielding phone calls or visits because no one called Mother and no one visited. Shirley could drive Mother's car and perhaps even take a short trip to Florida or some other warm state. Her opportunities appeared almost endless.

By noon, she had made her decision. Mother would rest, undisturbed, in the empty barn until spring. She would be well preserved because she would be quite frozen. If it was a cold spring, Mother could easily last through April at which time Shirley would have fled for parts unknown. She put on her boots and heavy parka, her hat, and her Thistledown gloves. She wrapped Mother in her salmon colored coat ordered from a Blair catalog. For a small woman, Mother was surprisingly heavy. By the time Shirley dragged her down the back steps and walked backwards to the barn, sweat was rolling from her armpits. The snow was over a foot deep, and Shirley was short. She was up to her knees in snow and the going was getting worse. Every few minutes she had to stop and catch Mother as she slipped from her grasp.

When she finally reached the barn, she dropped Mother in the snow. Mother's empty eyes stared at the sky, but Shirley didn't notice. She was intent upon opening the door, which was no easy task. Days earlier snow had melted from the roof, then frozen solid to the door's latch. Finally, after much tugging and foul language, the latch gave way, and Shirley was able to partially open the door. There was just enough room to squeeze through and drag Mother to her temporary resting place.

The interior of the barn was almost dark. There was one small window facing south. It was covered with dust, spider webs, straw, and rags. It took a few minutes for Shirley's eyes to adjust to the dimness. She put her arms underneath Mother's and dragged her to the stall farthest from the window. This stall had once belonged to Blanche, Mother's best and only Holstein. Shirley dumped the lifeless lump into the stall. She covered Mother with loose hay. Even if a neighbor kid came poking around, he would find nothing. Then Shirley latched the door and retraced her tracks back to the house.

The frying pan blow had not broken Mother's skin so there was no trace of blood. Shirley straightened the doilies on Mother's recliner and rearranged the multi-colored afghan. Everything looked neat and tidy, just the way she liked it. Shirley put Mother's black shawl in her bureau drawer and settled in a comfortable beige recliner with a copy of *Bartlett's Familiar Quotations* on her lap. She reached for the bottle of Bailey's Irish Cream and poured a generous amount into a crystal glass from Germany. She liked Mr. Bartlett and his book. She loved to memorize bits and pieces from the masters, but she rarely had time to devote to her hobby. Now she smiled as she sipped her drink and thought of the months ahead—months filled with Keats, Byron, Shakespeare, and dozens more. When Mr. Kelsey wasn't around, these dead men would make love to her during the late night hours. They would drink fine whiskey with her and court her until dawn. She opened the book and began reading until she tired of it. Then she began picturing what was happening in the barn. Her vivid imagination conjured the scene which was spot on.

It wasn't long before Mother awakened. She had a terrible headache and was very cold. "Where the hell am I?" she wondered aloud. "And what the hell am I doing here? Is it night or day? Must be night. Dark as a tar pit in here." She scratched the hay around her. "Barn," she said. "Smells like barn." She called for Ma, but there was no answer. "Where are you, sweet mother," she cried. "Help me. My head aches." When no help came, she crawled to the window and pulled herself upright. She grabbed the rags from the window. Now it made sense. She was at the barn. Probably Pa had sent her to check on one of the cows to see if the animal was ready to freshen. Sure, that was it. Pa was sick, and Ma was tending to him. She was 17 now, old enough to birth a calf by herself. But where was the cow?

She crawled to the barn door, but it was latched from the outside. A hoe leaned against the wall near the door. She held it in one hand while she crawled back to the window. With more strength than she realized was in her, she broke the windowpane with one thrust of the hoe. Then she smashed the remaining bits of glass. Mother was spry and surprisingly agile. She stepped on a bale of straw, stepped on the manger, and crawled out the window. She landed in a pile of snow. "Tracks," she said. "I'll follow these tracks." Mother was half-frozen by the time she crawled through the snow to the house. She made it up the back steps and scratched at the door. Shirley thought she heard something but reasoned it was only the wind. When Sis returned to Shirley's side, she stopped musing.

After the phone call, I returned to Shirley and held her hand. I sympathized with her as a good Christian should and suggested she continue her story. It's always been my belief it's best to get everything out in the open where it can be examined in detail so everyone knows the facts and understands the situation. Although Shirley hesitated, she blew her nose, wiped her tears, and finished her sad narrative.

Shirley thought Mother had returned to her bedroom when she was in the bathroom. So when she heard a noise at the back door, she assumed it was only the wind. This was unfortunate because unknown to Shirley, Mother was freezing to death. However, before she closed her eyes for the last time, she managed to strike a match to a box of oily rags on the porch. Eventually the flames entered the house. Shirley was lucky to escape with the clothes on her back and her book of famous quotations.

It was heartbreaking to see Shirley so distraught. Mr. Kelsey wanted to close the funeral parlor for the afternoon, but he didn't want to chase Shirley away while she was in such deep grief. "I'll never recover from this," she said. "Why would Mother do such a wicked thing? Why would she go out in the cold and set fire to all those rags on the back porch? Why would she want to kill me?" Shirley cried until I thought she was going to join dear Mother in her coffin.

Mr. Kelsey held her close to his chest and said comforting words. "There, there, Shirley," he crooned. "It's all over now. Mother is at peace and you are free. I mean fraught with fatigue. Things will look better tomorrow. We'll have to decide where you will live while the house is being repaired." I'm certain Mr. Kelsey's lips brushed Shirley's hair, but I couldn't swear to it, and I'm certainly not one to spread gossip.

"Shirley can stay with my Mother until more permanent arrangements are made," I said. "She's a widow and needs someone to look after her. I don't have time. I think she'll like Shirley." I patted her hand. "My dear, don't worry about a thing," I said.

Shirley thanked me. "You are too kind. I don't deserve you."

"Nonsense," I said. "It was the good Lord that brought us together, and it's the good Lord who'll see us through. Tomorrow we'll do some shopping. You need a new wardrobe."

"Did many things survive the flames?" Shirley asked.

"The fire department got there in time to save most everything in the bedroom farthest from the porch. The kitchen was pretty much gone except for one thing—an old cast iron frying pan. The fire marshal wanted to save it for you, but Mr. Kelsey thought it might give you nightmares, so the marshal threw it out with the rest of the rubble. Don't worry, though, because my Mother has plenty of them."

"Does your Mother have dementia?" Shirley asked. Her tears were gone, and she looked rather perky, almost like a young girl starting a new and exciting journey.

"I'm sorry to say but, yes, she does. Why?"

"No reason," Shirley said. "Does she quote poems?"

"Only one. It's called 'My Shadow.' Have you heard it?"

Shirley thought for a minute. "Can't say that I have," she said.

As I helped Shirley into my Crown Victoria, I told her Mother would gladly teach it to her. "That'll be nice," she said. "A poem is just what I need to grieve." She closed her eyes. A few snowflakes drifted down as I drove Shirley to her new home. I would make sure Mother's frying pan was in plain sight and easy to reach. I hummed a little tune as the car purred forward.

I love being a hairdresser at the funeral parlors. I meet the most interesting people. Even in their grief, most mourners look forward to a bright future.

The Upstairs Renter

I had just returned to Sault Ste. Marie from a trip to the Wild Atlantic Way along the southwest coast of Ireland, and I was consumed with an unexplainable sense of foreboding. A tour of the monastery ruins on Skellig Michael Island filled my mind with images of long-dead monks. I imagined their spirits returning to their ancient, isolated home, roaming through the ruins, seeking the solitude they had once known. I was doubtful their self-imposed seclusion had drawn them closer to God, but who was I to judge? Each man's journey to God is as different as the man himself yet in some insignificant way, I had convinced myself that separation from worldly distractions was the only way to purify my body, mind, and soul and discover the Great Infinite. It was something I yearned for—isolation and absolute silence—but instead, I found myself in the bitter grip of remorse and guilt.

I was confused and depressed when word reached me of the unexpected death of my girlfriend, Emma. I immediately fled back to the states from the desolate cottage I had rented in County Kerry, but instead of finding comfort in my friends, I found only disappointment. It didn't matter who I was with or where I was because my thoughts followed me. They were driving me mad. Was I the reason Emma had taken her life? Was I to blame? Was I going to live in torment the rest of my life because I could not bring myself to wed a woman who never stopped talking? Why would I, a man who demanded a quiet environment, yoke myself to a chatterbox? Had I, in a moment of mental fatigue, made promises to her I could not keep?

Upon my return, I emptied the apartment Emma and I had shared near Lake Superior State University and moved into a flat on Kimball Street just off Spruce. It was a neighborhood in flux so it matched my state of mind. I recalled the words of the landlord, a Mr. Lybac, when he handed me the keys. "The upstairs renter is a quiet young man," he said. "He's studying to be a physicist. No loud parties, music, or drama of any kind. I had to turn out the last renters due to the noise."

I assured him that as a writer, I too, demanded a peaceful place in which to create. We shook hands. I signed a year's lease and settled in.

I began writing with a great sense of expectation. My recent experiences lay heavily on my mind, and I wrote with a fury I hadn't felt since the death of Emma a few weeks earlier. The ancient Irish ruins around Caherdaniel, where I had stayed, fed my imagination. I was consumed with a desire to write about the people who had once breathed the salty air in their now-deserted stone homes. I felt an overwhelming need to recreate them. Their passing, whether through a spirit of hope as they left for America or out of despair as they cast themselves into the Atlantic, would be for me to decide. I would resurrect the dead. If they were incomplete entities, at least I would create a feeling, an aura of their lives. I closed myself off from everything but my writing, giving it all the passion of my youth—I was only 27—as well as my grief.

For days I did not leave my rooms. I awoke early, opened the window in my study and breathed the cold, sharp October air before returning to my typewriter. I had not seen the upstairs renter, but the sounds he made were comforting and reminded me of my childhood and our renter. Mother and I lived in a two family flat on Stopel, a tree-lined street on Detroit's west side. Father was killed in World War II leaving Mother a small life insurance policy. She immediately purchased the sturdy brick house and rented the upstairs to an elderly man. One night he died in his sleep and wasn't discovered until the smell of him drifted into our flat. I was five years old at the time. Occasionally I get a whiff of something that reminds me of that renter. It is not a pleasant memory, but I've come to accept the fact that many things from our childhood are unpleasant when we look back at them through the unfiltered lens of adulthood.

Every day I heard the upstairs renter as he walked around his flat. Each room was a mirror image of the other. I felt I was living with an invisible twin on top of my head. Lybac had not exaggerated the man's need for quiet. Had it not been for the scraping of his chair or the sound of his footsteps pacing the uncarpeted floors, I should have thought myself quite alone in the house. At first I welcomed the quiet as a pleasant change from the clutter of noise, but as autumn evenings wrapped themselves around me, I felt the need to share my thoughts with someone. The quiet of the house was settling on me like a shroud. It crept into my rooms and reminded me of the emptiness I felt when I first saw the Skellig ruins, the crumbling castles, and the abandoned cottages along my daily walk to the Atlantic. A growing melancholy began entering me that I found increasingly hard to shed until a gust of wind from the window interrupted my thoughts and scattered the notes from my desk. I hastily retrieved them and closed the window, locking out the northwest wind threatening to blow the early morning sun from Michigan to Mexico. A storm was brewing along the horizon just waiting for its cue to send neighborhood youngsters running for their homes and the warmth of their living rooms where Saturday morning cartoons blared from television sets. I watched dry leaves skip down Kimball, chasing each other in an endless, no-win race. My whistling tea kettle beckoned me to the kitchen.

It wasn't long before I heard the upstairs renter's step on the back stairs. I opened my door and hurried out to greet him. "Hello," I called as he descended. "I'm Thatcher Grange." A tall, slender man brushed past me, ignoring my outstretched hand. Without a word, he opened the door and disappeared into the wind. Although I was miffed at his rebuff, I dismissed him as an ignorant bumpkin, poured hot water over the teabag in my cup, and returned to my study. I started writing about Bunratty Castle in County Clare. Although outwardly it was magnificent, the interior was disappointing. The place had given me a chill which was not the result of the damp but of the intrusion. Tourists crammed into the dining room where tables were stacked high with platters of the warm flesh from dead animals. I was acutely aware of how ridiculous we looked pretending to be participants in a meal from the past. Eating flesh akin to that consumed by dead Celts disturbed my sense of honor and decency. Before the chewing began, I left the room and roamed the grounds. I had to distance myself from the sight of gluttonous humanity.

I returned to my writing but found it difficult to concentrate. The encounter with the upstairs renter had rattled me. I preferred my own company and had no interest in meeting someone who guarded his privacy as much as I did, but I despised rudeness. I turned on the radio. The announcer thundered some nonsense about pantyhose. I turned the dial and another voice encouraged me to buy an ointment for hemorrhoids, an ailment foreign to me. Disgusted, I turned off the radio and put an album on my stereo. I was usually inspired by Vivaldi's "The Four Seasons," but instead of "Autumn" providing inspiration, it provoked anger. The violins seemed to mimic what was happening outside my window. They reminded me of the storm that had greeted me when I arrived at my lodgings in Ireland's isolated countryside.

Gale force winds blew off the Atlantic. They downed power lines as if they were toothpicks, uprooted trees, and forced animals to seek shelter wherever they could or be blown away like tissue paper. I switched off the stereo and put Vivaldi back in his jacket. I dressed and headed for the door. A blast of wind hit my face and a few drops of rain sprinkled around me. The weather was raw, and I walked with no purpose. My aimless drifting led me to the Soo's oldest cemetery, Maple Ridge, on Ashmun Street. Since my youth, tombstones had fascinated me. I sought the oldest ones and talked to the dead as if they were my companions.

It was late when I returned to my flat. I was refreshed and inspired. I added page upon page to my manuscript, writing long into the night. My characters consumed me, draining my strength while simultaneously giving me renewed vigor. I borrowed scenes from the ruins of Skellig Michael and wove them into fictitious memoirs of people who had once called the island home. I became absorbed with their lives, twisting and shaping them into tangible beings. My characters breathed inside my mind until they overpowered me with their reality. Their silent ears listened as I put them on paper. Their dead eyes watched as I re-created them. I felt their approval and thankfulness as I breathed life into them. Fatigue overtook me as the night wore on, but I could not stop.

Once the work began to take shape, every moment of the following days and nights found me at my typewriter. Often I felt I would burst from the sheer power my characters possessed over me. I knew my hours of typing disturbed the upstairs renter. Instead of knocking on my door and asking me to refrain from typing during the midnight hours, he pounded the floor above me. Sometimes the slam of his study door created a splash of noise that reverberated throughout my rooms. When I could no longer stand the sounds he was inflicting upon me, I stopped using my typewriter and started writing with yellow pencils and legal pads. I couldn't abide his anger at the sound of my Adler's keys hitting the paper. I was convinced he purposely broke my concentration by scraping his chair on the floor.

Added to the scraping was his endless cough. When it ceased for a moment, it was replaced by the slap of his footsteps as he walked miles in the space of a few rooms. He paced for hours. I willed my thoughts back to my work and filled the air around me with visions of the Kerry Coast ghost, but it was not that ghost I saw, but Emma's. My pencil scratched on the pad, as if moving by itself, going faster and faster, flying over the pages until, overcome with anxiety, I moved to the living room to escape the noise coming from above.

The renter followed me. I sat on my rocking chair and heard his rocker creaking above. Every time I moved, he moved. I felt his presence enter me. I wrote with a lighter touch to mask the scratch of the pencil. Then without warning, his rocking stopped and he began prowling. His feet slapped the floor with hard, quick jabs. I covered my ears to silence the racket puncturing them, but it was a useless gesture. Finally he stopped walking, and I felt the quiet from him flow down the stairs and move into my rooms. It pushed me aside. I watched as it claimed the chair next to mine. Flames from the fireplace illuminated it. It glowed, it sighed, it labeled my possessions as its own and when the rocking above me started again, it demanded peace.

The renter coughed again. I imaged great wads of phlegm choking him. The thought repulsed me. I put down my pencil as the quiet crept around my neck and demanded silence, but what could I do? I had already unplugged the radio, the stereo, the clocks, the refrigerator, the toaster. I had the telephone removed and the doorbell disconnected, but I could not silence the coughing from above or the wind. October had drifted into November. Wind howled, rattling the windows and shaking the house, sending loose shingles sailing through grey skies. Day after day, it would not stop. Upstairs I heard the renter coughing, pacing, and apparently blaming me for nature's roar. I buried myself deeper in my work, not daring to leave my rooms lest the closing of a door further anger him.

On Thanksgiving Day he departed at dawn. The wind died and a tangible calm spread itself throughout the house. My holiday meal was a tuna fish sandwich and black coffee. It was a feast as I had not eaten in days. My writing consumed me. In the silence of the empty house, my work and I became one. The renter did not return until after Christmas. The familiar scrape of his study chair filled me with joy, and I turned the quiet over to him, making it his responsibility to keep any intruding noises at bay. I had not slept in days. My eyes gladly gave up their vigil. The softness of my mattress comforted me. I was almost asleep when I heard the squeaking of the bedsprings from above. Stop torturing me, I yelled silently to the ceiling. Give me peace. When sleep finally overtook me, it was a restless one and I fought it, the bed covers rustling loudly in my ears.

I heard snow falling when I awoke. I dragged myself to the bathroom. My eyes were sunken like two stones in gray mud. My frame was too thin. My beard needed trimming as did my fingernails, but the snap of scissors and the snip of nail clippers had become intolerable, not only to him above, but to myself as well. I walked slowly to my study, sliding my feet along the bare floor. Upstairs I saw him crouching, waiting for the noise to filter up, waiting to tell Lybac and have me thrown out with the New Year. I had to find a way to remain quiet and still complete my manuscript.

By now his cough had become constant. Raw drafts seeped through the old house, seeped into his bones. Did I dare venture to his rooms with aspirin and cough suppressant in hand? Yes, I must. He did not answer my knock, but I left my offerings outside his door and quickly retreated. I knew he watched me, for I felt his eyes boring into me as I glided down the stairs. When I flicked the light switch, the sound traveled through the ceiling and he switched his twice, the noise blasting around me. I wrote with crayons, for the scratch of the pencil reverberated like the boom of a canon and his chair scraped heavily as a warning.

My rooms were heated only by the fireplace now, the hiss and bang of the crashing furnace created a fury in him greater than I could bear. Even the tea kettle's whistle was ear-splitting and I dispensed with it, making instant coffee with hot water from the kitchen tap. A winter fly buzzed in my ears until I pounded them. At night I put poison out for stray cats. I could not endure their howls. I wrote by candlelight but even the dripping wax was a screeching ejaculation. Whatever I did was not enough for the upstairs renter. He pounded the floor above me, scraped his chair across it, crashed pots and pans together, and I sought greater levels of silence.

By March, I had confined myself to a chair in the living room. I crept to the bathroom, but kept the kitchen, bedroom, and study doors locked. Still, I heard him upstairs, endlessly pacing, endlessly turning the pages of his textbooks. I saw him facing invisible scientists, demanding them to be quiet. I kept my windows closed to keep out the street sounds and blaring chatter of growing grass and spring flowers. My room was crowded with paper from my writing. My novel was almost finished. I had taken my experiences of crumbling castles and cottage ruins and the pounding waves of the Atlantic and woven them into a crisscross pattern that dipped and flowed and worked. My body had become a shell. I was frayed, drained, weak, but at peace with what I had created for it was good. Emma would have been proud.

One rainy April evening I heard the silence creep down the stairs. I hid in my coat closet. It waited patiently, knowing I would eventually acknowledge it. I heard it floating through my living room. I opened the door and saw it resting on my manuscript. "Get off," I screamed. The sound of my words was a cacophony—a shrill, blatant, thunder in my ears. The renter smashed his book to the floor and stomped his feet as the scrape of his chair drove deep trenches into the wood. I grabbed the manuscript from underneath the silence and clutched it to my breast. I got the broom and began swinging the plastic bristles at the invisible intruder until I sank to the floor, feeling the silence seep through my skin and hearing my shrieks echo throughout the room.

For hours nothing moved. Not air nor light nor dust nor sound. I thought the renter would be pleased, but when dark came, he started moving things, pushing heavy furniture across the room, and banging the floor. Louder and louder the clamor grew. Long into the night, I realized I was conscious of nothing but the flow of his presence. Time stood still, yet it flew. As if in a dream, the silence walked to my kitchen, took a butcher knife from the drawer, and ascended the stairs. The door was open. I watched as the silence sliced through the renter's neck until a bright red substance spread itself across the floor.

The following day I sent my novel to my publisher who accepted it with few revisions. I looked forward to the financial success it would bring. I enjoyed the peace of my home and became friends with the silence. As the weeks passed, I wondered when the smell of the upstairs renter would penetrate my rooms. I made a decision. Before the stench invaded the street and neighbors notified Lybac, I would join my nameless friend. Death would bring us the peace and quiet we both cherished but had failed to find in life.

Departure would be a welcome relief, but before I could find the knife that had killed him, the silence found it. With one quick thrust, I saw Emma smiling at me and offering her hand, but I was gone before I could grab it. I ran for the door and raced down the street. I stopped when I reached the bar located in the basement of the Delmar Hotel & Restaurant. For the first time in a year, I thrust myself into the midst of merriment. I reveled in the sounds of laughter, the band's loud music, the pounding of feet as couples danced, the clang of beer glasses, and the shouting for a waitress to bring another round. The absolute bliss of being among the living enfolded me. It was more than the spirits in my glass intoxicating me. It was life. Thoughts of Skellig Michael, dead monks, Mr. Lybac, and the upstairs renter fled from my mind. I smiled

Memories of Rose

My name is Howard Beech. I'm an old man living in God's country, otherwise known as the Eastern Upper Peninsula. My little corner of this haven is called Cottage Park, ten miles or so south of Sault Ste. Marie. It's almost midnight, December 31, 1999, and since I'm alone and feeling a bit downhearted, I've a mind to share my thoughts with you. The New Year's coming in cold and hard, blowing and storming and making a right mess of the roads, tossing cars into ditches, smothering rich and poor alike underneath a mountain of snow. I heard there's a hundred car pile-up on northbound I-75 near Grayling. Five dead, many injured. I listened to the radio until the battery ran down, then I stirred the coals in the woodstove and made myself a cup of tea and a piece of toast piled high with last summer's strawberry jam. Then I headed to bed. I tried reading for a while but just couldn't get interested in anything and the light from the kerosene lamp burned my eyes.

I get the jitters listening to all the millennium talk. Every station I pulled in had some young pup jabbering on about 1999 marking the end of the world. Seems like everybody's looking forward to 2000 when all the computers crash or Jesus Christ Himself comes back. You hear things you don't see when all you've got are your ears to depend upon. You don't get the feel for what a man's saying when you're watching him on TV. You're busy looking at his tie or what's going on in the background or the pictures they're showing or that little piece of snot dangling from the corner of his nose as it moves in and out when he breathes. But when all you've got is the radio, you hear what's not being said as much as what is. You can tell by the way a feller's voice highers and lowers whether or not he's believing what he's saying. A man's character comes through his voice when you take away his face. The only time I watch the news is when I visit a neighbor and that isn't often.

I'm having a hard time falling asleep tonight. I wrapped a flannel sheet around me and my first cover is Ma's old quilt. There's no heat in it now. It's full of holes, but her hands worked it so I keep it. On top of the quilt is the Army blanket and on top of that is a bedspread my dear wife, Rose, knit for me. Every winter for more than 50 years, I've slept with two women and the Army on my back, and I'm none the worse for it as near as I can tell. If I still can't get warm, I call the cat and dog and they pile in with me. Jeb's at my feet now, snoring like the lazy hound dog he is. Muffin's curled next to him.

I hear the wind howling. I've tried to like that sound but just can't reach far enough into my memory to pull out any good connection between that noise and happiness. It's a mournful wail. It's all but shaking the house. I know it's blowing snow, banking the front door so that by morning I'll have to go out the back and shovel a path to the front. The wind's coming from the southeast. It cuts through the house like a hot knife cuts through butter. I turned up the oil stove a couple notches today and usually that warms the place real good, but nothing's a match for the southeasterly. I built this house for Rose and me, but God didn't let her live long enough to enjoy it.

I don't mind getting old, but I sure don't like getting old alone. It's times like this—Christmas, end of the year, birthdays—that I miss her the most. If she had lived, the place would be full of grandkids by now, all piling over each, all looking for a gift from grandpa. I'd have liked that. Rose and I only had a few years together before the consumption wore her out. She was sick, knew it as soon as I saw her when the Army let me go and I beat a path for home. She had consumption and pretended it was just a cold she couldn't shake. I went along with her. I guess most of us believe what we want to, not what's laid before our eyes, plain as day. She got better that summer and fall, even hung on during the winter, but come the first good spring thaw in 1947, she went downhill fast.

I sat by her side for hours, getting up only to stoke the fire or take care of the livestock then I'd come back and hold her hand or stroke her hair. We pretended we had years ahead of us and planned the garden and the baby that might come. We even planned a nursery with no north windows, but it wasn't meant to be. Rose left me early one April morning, slipped away while I was stirring the coals to life in the kitchen stove. Slipped away as fast and soft as a newborn kitten. Never said a word, just left like dying was the easiest thing in the world. When the earth thawed, I laid her next to Ma and Pa at the Riverside Cemetery in the Soo. I wanted her on our land, but the officials put up such a stink that after I waked her at our house, I gathered her in my arms one last time and let her go.

Boy, I don't like the sound of that wind. It stirs up too many memories. It's making Jeb nervous, too. He jumped off the bed, but Muffin stayed put. I try not to move during the night so I don't disturb them, but I stiffen up if I stay in one position too long so every few hours when a joint tightens up, I turn and the critters turn with me. Muffin usually stretches her legs, goes to the kitchen and nibbles at her food then jumps back in bed and purrs until she falls asleep. But neither me or the critters can sleep tonight. The clock by my bed is ticking and the hands read half-past one. Already the New Year's getting old. In the blink of an eye, a year's gone. I wonder what will happen next. Nothing, I bet. Nothing ever happens when you're expecting it. It's when you're all snug and cozy and life looks good and you've got a little money hidden in a sock and your health's with you, that's when disaster strikes. So, no, I don't expect anything special to happen in 2000. Wait a few years is what I say. That's when the real trouble will come.

I keep up with what's going on in the world by listening to my radio. I don't have a phone. The way I figure it, a man becomes slave to whatever gadget he owns. The one concession I've made to the modern world is my truck. It isn't new, but I make sure it's in good running condition and what I can't fix I take to one of the garages in town. I've spray painted that truck three times, but the rust comes back and eats away the frame. In a year or so I'll trade it in for another new used one. A chocolate brown Ford with an orange stripe running down the side. Folks will see me coming from a quarter mile away and put on a fresh pot of coffee.

Rose believed in Jesus. Golly, but my mind's jumping from one thing to another. She read the Bible and I got interested in it too. I read it for almost two years after she left me, but then I put it aside. I wasn't what you might call mad at God. I just couldn't figure out why He took my wife. I asked Him over and over to let her live. I begged, pleaded, cried, yelled, and begged again, but it didn't do any good. I tried to figure out how her death could give meaning to my life, but I still haven't found an answer. After those two years of trying to make sense of her early passing, I closed the Bible and put it away. Not far, though. It's right on the bedstand. Sometimes in the middle of the night, I reach out and put my hand on it, but I don't open it. If God didn't answer my prayers for Rose, maybe I was just praying to the wind. I pull the covers over my head. The cold just cracked the window on the north side of the room. I'm used to the house cracking but never the windows. Must be at least 30 below, more when you consider the wind. There it goes again. A window in the kitchen this time. I should get up and see if they're really cracked or just making a noise, but it's too cold to get out of bed. I'll check them in the morning.

How can time go so fast during the day and so slow at night? I'm watching the hands crawl around the clock. I don't like nights like this. There's too much going on in my mind. Seems to me we just go through a lot of heartache and then we die. Some people's trials last longer than others, and some bring troubles upon themselves, but no matter, we all have a cross to carry. I've thought and thought about this living business many a night as I lay here feeling every ache and pain and wondering if this is the night I'm going to join my Rose. One time a sharp pain cut through me and I got scared. I drove to the neighbor's house and asked the husband to take me to the Soo's War Memorial Hospital. Thought my heart was giving out. I've said for years it was alright with me to be called at any time, but when I thought it was really happening, I cut tail and ran for help. Old Bates, the neighbor-husband loaded me in his van and hauled me as far as the emergency door. Then he went back home. Those people in white coats started poking and testing and x-raying everything when all I wanted was a heart test. After five hours of torture, I told them to call Old Bates to come and get me. Now when I feel a twitch, I ignore it.

Rose fancied horses so I always have some around the barn. I get them from an auction in Marion below the Mackinac Bridge. I go with a feller named Flood and pick out the sickest and most abused and load them in the trailer and head home. Some die along the way and when we arrive at my place, we get out the tractor and scoop and bury them. The live ones are herded into the pasture. The sickest are led into clean stalls and given feed and water. By the time we're finished, it's four in the morning. Flood comes in and I fire up the stove and fix bacon and eggs and lots of hot, strong coffee. While we eat, we rehash the auction. Then before he heads home, he sleeps for a few hours on a cot by the stove in the kitchen. He nods off as soon as his head hits the pillow, but it takes me a long time to sleep. I keep thinking about all those poor horses and mules heading for the glue factories. One time there were seven jet black colts all from the same farm, all lively and kicking up their heels, half-starved and scared. They came in after I'd already bought enough to fill the trailer. It made me sick I couldn't bring them home. I told Flood next time I'll rent a truck and trailer in Marion so I don't ever again have to live with the memory of seven sets of jet black eyes wide with excited anticipation, not knowing they were going to their death.

Well, I must have slept awhile. My right hand's gone numb again. It gets so heavy, it wakes me up. If it isn't the hand, it's the cold. If it isn't the cold, it's the cat jumping on my head. If it isn't the cat, it's Jeb licking my face. If it isn't Jeb, it's a wolf howling. If it isn't the howling, it's the barn owl hooting. If it isn't the owl, it's the ringing in my ears. They've rung all my life and I don't imagine they'll ever let up. It's like a hum that gets louder and louder until I want to scream, but I can't fix it so I've got to live with it. I can't turn it off like the radio because how do you turn off the noise in your ears? For the most part, though, aside from the ringing and the odd heart pain, I'm in pretty good shape for 79. Broke my ankle last spring and that almost did me in. Flood and the wife moved downstate, but he came running as soon as he got my letter. He took care of me just like my Rose would have. I sure missed him when he left. I hired a neighbor kid to plant my garden, but all that came up were beets, beets, and more beets. I don't know what he did with the rest of the seeds I gave him, but beets were all I got.

I'm wide awake now. I try to remember Rose's face, but to tell the truth, if it wasn't for her picture hanging on the front room wall, I couldn't properly recollect what she looked like except for her long yellow hair. I built my life around hers. Loved her since we were little kids. Used to ride my pony through the fields to her house just off M-129. Her Pa, a Swede they called Stringbean, sold oats. I remember one time my Pa bought some from him, and Stringbean bit an oat in half just so Pa wouldn't get more than he paid for. Thankfully, Rose didn't get those cheap Stringbean genes. Must be something nagging at me tonight. Something more than the storm is making me restless. Something way back in my mind must be trying to get out. Four-thirty. In another hour, I'll stir the embers in the stove and get a fire going. Then I'll get the coffee going while I fry eggs and sausage for breakfast. I might slice a biscuit and slather it with butter and jam. Then I'll head outside and do some shoveling before I feed and water the horses.

I listen for the wind, but it seems to have died down so that's good. I think the storm pretty much blew itself out because I don't hear any noise from the weather. If I put everything out of my mind, maybe, just maybe, sleep will come in with the New Year. I close my eyes and who do I see? Why, my beautiful Rose, smiling and waving and running to greet me. I touch my face and brush away the tears that escape like they always do. When I open my eyes, Rose is gone.

Summer Will Not Come Again

Old man, why do you sit in the sun and wear a heavy flannel shirt on such a warm August day in Gardenville? Get up and tend to your fields that lie fallow as they wait for the tractor and mower or manure spreader and seeder to give them new life. Don't you know you're not dead yet? That life still runs through your blue veins? Sing me a song as you did when I was a babe and there was no worry about hospitals and worse. When I knew you would never go to a strange place where I cannot follow.

All summer Dad sat in the blue metal chair by the front door and rocked. "Can't reach my cane," he would call to my daughter as she played in the yard. Honey would race to him, place the cane into his knotted hands and pat his knees, then run back to her play. He watched as she danced around the yard—danced among the petunias and decorative white wooden fences and yellow plastic hens and ducks, and he would think of his own youth when there was no dancing, no happiness only sorrow and hard work. Honey knew he watched her, for although only a mere child of four, she knew, and she watched him when he stopped watching her and slept in his chair. Once she watched a horsefly buzz around him and land on his hand. She waited for him to awaken and when he slept on, she slapped it and watched it fly away. She was afraid she had awakened her grandfather, but no, he only stirred and returned to his dreams.

Is this what it means to be old? I thought.

Get up, old man, and show me that you are still alive. Okay, okay, if you must wear the flannel shirt at least roll up the sleeves. Don't cross your legs like that, at the knee, like an old woman, but spread them wide as you did years ago when you hunched forward and told stories that kept us begging for more even as we, your offspring, huddled together because your stories were scary. Must you rest your hands on your cane like that, one crossed upon the other? Oh, that cane. I remember when you found the tree limb in the woods behind the house, how you brought it home and polished it until it glistened and then how you put it away until age demanded you lean upon it. Don't die on me, old man, for you still have much to tell me.

He watched as Honey brought his rocks. "What's this one called, Grandpa?"

"Well, let's see. That black shiny stuff running through it is called mica. And the white stuff that sparkles in the sun is quartz. And the pink is granite. I forget what the yellow is. Maybe fool's gold."

"Mica, quartz, fool's gold. What's granite?"

"Comes from the ground. Takes millions of years to get made. Bring me the rock book and we'll read all about them."

Skipping, running, he followed her with his sea blue eyes. Then they left her and rested on the woods, and he singled out the opening in them where he had fed the cattle in winter. He could still make it out and if he looked hard enough he could see the Herefords attacking the bales with their horns, throwing the loose hay into the air, anxious to get to the sweet middle. Eventually they would eat what they had first cast aside, but that was later in the day when the inside was gone. He could see the calves, too, jumping behind their mothers and butting each other with their tiny horns. The cattle were gone now. He was too old to take care of them. Too old to take off hay and fill the mow with winter bales. A breeze told him to unroll the shirtsleeves.

"Here, Grandpa. Read."

Get up, old man. There's work to be done. Or if you don't want to work right now, well then, just sharpen the mower blade so it will be ready when you want to cut the fields. No? Not now? Well, maybe later. Please don't fall asleep again. I just got here. Talk to me. Old man, I know you hear me. You always hear me. Where's your cap? I don't know. Wherever you left it. The cattle? You know they're gone. They've been gone for years. I know the barn's in good shape, but the cows are gone. It's okay. Cry.

"Read."

"It says here granite was melted rock that hardened way beneath the earth and after a million years or so, it's taken from the ground and..."

"Maybe read later." Honey skipped away to find Granny and follow her. "Grandpa's old, isn't he?" she asked.

"Not that old, but he's ill. Remember when he went to the hospital and you couldn't see him for a week?"

"Yes. Is he sick now?"

"Yes, but we'll talk about that later. Let's see if any of the radishes are ready to pick."

Dad watched as his wife of 40 years held Honey's hand and they walked to the garden. Every year, for as long as he could recall, Mom planted the garden in the same spot. He tried to tell her the ground would yield more if she gave it a rest and planted the garden elsewhere, but he couldn't tell her anything. So every spring he plowed up the same earth and put compost on it, and the rich black fertilizer of long dead cows made the earth yield bountiful crops. So he guessed she was right about that, too.

They were on their knees now, Mom and Honey, searching for radishes, pulling up fat red ones and brushing them free of soil. Mom's chestnut hair was gray now. She was thin, too, much thinner than last year. Her green eyes had moved further into their sockets. Still, Dad saw her as the young bride and gentle taskmaster she had always been, intent upon monitoring his activities. She was more cautious now. More thoughtful of him lest he do too much and cause his heart to fail again. He shifted in the hard chair. Skip, the cat, nuzzled his ankles. He reached down and scratched its head. Skip took this gesture as an invitation and jumped on his lap. Dad lost hold of his cane. It clattered when it hit the cement.

"You okay?" Mom yelled. "You okay?" She left Honey and ran from the garden.

"Of course, I'm okay." He grabbed the cane and winced as pain passed through his heart. Then, ignoring Mom's concerned clucking, he hobbled to the garden. She told him to be careful. "It's too hot out there," she yelled. "Get back on the porch." She was to his back and he could not, would not hear. "You'll kill yourself in that hot sun. Do you hear me? Come back on the porch. Come back." Honey skipped off and joined him.

"I found a blueberry, Grandpa," she said as she handed it to him. "Here." She placed the tiny berry in the hollow of his hand. "And here's another one. Look. And here's two more. I found a good patch." She knelt in the middle of it. He watched as the squashed berries stained her white shorts. "Look over there. Lots of them." She pushed the bushes every which way to get to the fruit. "Look." She handed him five tiny berries, three with the tips still green. "I did good, didn't I?" He leaned down and kissed the top of her head.

That's right, old man. Kiss the young one. Feel the love that flows from her life to yours. Know that she is part of you, and that when you die she will remain. And what's that I see? Another tear? Twice today? Tears from the eyes that have been dry all my life? Well, it's okay. It's not a bad thing to cry. But it's too hot, so best get out of the sun.

"You did good," Dad said and took the berries and put them in his mouth. Honey watched him chew. She gave him more. He ate all she offered, even the green ones. Even the stems that mingled with the fruit. "Good," he said. She wrapped her arms around his knees. He patted her head. They walked towards the pea patch. "Only blossoms on most of them," he said. "But soon they'll be ready. See that tiny pod forming at the tip of the blossom? Soon we'll be shelling peas on the porch and your grandmother will be yelling at us, telling us not to eat too many."

"Granny yells a lot."

I watched them walk through the garden, examining beans, tomatoes, onions, corn, beets, and carrots. I watched and wondered why he had never taken my hand and walked with me through the gardens of my youth. Watched and wondered if he were walking with me now through my child. Watched and wondered when he had started walking so slowly. Mom sat next to me on the porch swing. I could feel her fear. "Too hot for him to be anywhere but on the porch," she said. "Get back here," she yelled at Dad.

"The cows are gone," he told Honey.

"I know."

"The sun's hot."

"I like it. Can we go to the beach?"

"Not today."

A breeze stirred.

"Why not?"

A breeze stirred and the corn silks waved.

"It's too hot."

A breeze stirred and the corn silks waved and he felt more pain in his chest.

Get out of the sun, old man. When did your hair turn white? When did you become thin? I don't remember you being so thin or your shoulders being so bony or your chest so small. I thought you were taller. When did you lose your height? And that scar over your right eye. Is that the one you got when you were splitting wood and a chip flew and lodged in your eyebrow? Those green workman's pants. The plaid flannel shirts. Slippers? No steel toe boots? Get out of the sun, old man.

"But I want to go to the beach. Why can't we go, Grandpa?"

"Get back here. My God, Kate," Mom said. "He's walking towards the woods. Come back. Come back." We raced towards him.

And he felt his chest sear from the weight of white hot flames and it felt good. He walked faster, throwing away the cane and soaring towards the trees. He could hear now and the legs felt fine and his eyes were clear and he saw her face before him and those of his children and he was flying now and the pain was nothing compared to the freedom it gave him. And he drank in the hot summer air as he felt the heat grow in his chest and he thought he heard someone calling him, but then the heat was upon him and he gave himself to it until it burned out and was replaced by peaceful drops of rain falling on his soul.

Old man, old man, no more will you sit in the sun and wrap your heavy flannel shirt around your thin shoulders. No more will you hold the hand of my daughter or brush off the hand of your wife. No more will you rest your head against the flank of a cow as you milk her. No more will you grease the mower or load bales of hay onto the elevator leading to the mow. No more will you see another sunset. Old man, old man. No. Father. Dearest, precious, Father.

"Grandpa fell," Honey said. "Mama, Granny, help me pick him up. I found more blueberries. Get up, Grandpa. Please get up." She held out her little hand to him. A gentle breeze picked up her words. They floated away and mingled with the spirit of Grandpa.

Long-Suffering Edith

The early August morning was quiet at Les Cheneaux. No cars sped down M-134. No boat whistles sounded as the sailors tightened the hatches and left the Carmeuse quarry in Cedarville and glided east on Lake Huron heading for Lake Michigan and Burns Harbor in Indiana. Even the owls made no sound, and the crickets were silent. The peaceful night passed, broken only by my daughter's cries that became whimpers as they drifted through her wall into our bedroom. Phil slept on, but I couldn't. I waited, hoping Connie's nightmare would pass, but it didn't. I wish there was something I could do to ease whatever is tormenting her, but I haven't been able to help. I can't reach her and let her know how much we love her. If only she were more like her sister, Nancy, strong and cheerful, but Connie is silent and sad, always brooding about something.

Phil reaches for me, but I turn away. I've lost all interest in making love. It happened so gradually over the past year I hardly noticed my desire leaving until one day I realized it was gone. Phil doesn't understand. He courted me for months, pressuring me into marriage, but I balked at the idea. When I realized I was with child, the decision was taken out of my hands. We were married 13 years ago in a tiny chapel that's now one of the ghost buildings facing the lake. It was a windy March morning. A wild morning that matched my mood. I was too young to be a bride, let alone a mother. I wasn't ready, but what else could I do? If I had held my ground and not given in to temptation, I would still have my freedom.

When I was a little girl, I often heard Ma crying at night when she thought I was asleep. She had five stillborn births. I'd listen as she said the name of each dead infant. She rhymed them off like days of the week and asked God to protect them until she could join them. She prayed all the time about everything, but what I remember most is that she prayed to die. I was eight or nine when I asked her why. I remember she gave me a strange look. She put down her darning needle and folded her hands.

"Life is hard," she said. "And it doesn't get any easier the longer you live. Might as well go home to the Lord sooner as later." I can still see her sitting in her rocker with a ball of navy blue yarn and a wooden darning egg resting on her lap. When tears rolled down my cheeks she patted my hand and told me not to worry, that God would work things out. Then she went back to her darning and rocking. That rocking chair was her prized possession, given to her by her mother. It stands in our bedroom now. Sometimes I think Ma is watching me, sitting there in the corner, pointing a sharp needle at me, cursing me for giving into lust and marrying a poor man instead of a rich one.

Phil reaches for me again. He slips his arm around my waist and rubs my belly. He whispers in his sleep, something about wanting another baby. He wants a son, but I'm afraid. Nancy was a breech birth, and I almost died with her. I was terrified to have another child, but then a year later Connie came along and the 36 hour labor for her almost finished me. Unlike Nancy, who was round and chubby, Connie was long and thin. She was perfect, too, except for the birthmark on her forehead, a red mark in the shape of a sword. The mark gradually faded, but when she cries or gets angry, the sword flames red. I feel the warmth from Phil's body as mine arouses his. I've learned to love him over the years. He's a good man, but I'm not ready to be a wife in the physical sense. I'm tired. Tired of everything. Everyone wants a piece of me. They think I can fix all their problems as easily as the priest gives absolution—with the wave of his hand and the sign of the cross. If it were that easy, I would be glad to oblige all of them.

"You awake?" Phil asks. He's pressing into me.

"Yes. Connie had another nightmare." His hand leaves my belly and his strong fingers encircle mine. He squeezes them.

"Did you talk to the priest about her? Isn't there something he can do?" His breath is sweet. I know he rinsed his mouth with the schnapps from his nightstand. The concern in his voice brings tears to my eyes. Connie is his favorite.

"Yes, you know I have, but he says he watches her eyes on Sunday morning and they're blank. It's like her soul is gone. He thinks something happened to her, but she won't confess it and he doesn't know what to do anymore than we do. Please, Phil. Not now." He ignores me, his need for me greater than his desire to honor my wishes. When it's over, I cry. "Don't," he says and tries to comfort me. "Maybe the seed will take, and our son will come with the spring. It would be a new beginning for us." He kisses my lips, turns from me, and goes back to sleep.

I feel his sperm sticking to my thighs and hope his phantom son is sliding down my legs. I wish I could avoid intercourse. That's all it is to me. A conjugal act I'm required to perform for his pleasure. My passion is gone as is my desire to be an obedient wife. When I was young, I read all the English novels I could find. I imagined my life would be filled with adventure and travel that would inspire me to be a writer. Now I only have enough energy to write the grocery list. I no longer have dreams. Sometimes I think Connie will fulfill them. She's a loner and is always reading. She spends too much time by herself. Sometimes she rides her bicycle down the dusty back roads and is gone for hours. She never tells me where she goes or what she does or if she meets someone.

I close my eyes and listen to the silence of the upstairs. Connie's whimpering has stopped and both girls are deep in sleep. With each breath, I feel their childhood slipping away. I long to hold it for them, but instead, perhaps I help it disappear through my inability to express happiness with my lot in life. Maybe in the long run, it's better that way. There's tension between me and their father and when he drinks too much things get worse. Last winter he was so drunk a neighbor drove him home from Snows Bar in Cedarville and dumped him on the front porch. If the dog hadn't barked, I don't think I would have heard him. I was so engrossed in a book, he might have frozen to death if it's possible for a drunk to freeze. I awakened the girls, and we hauled Phil in. Nancy thought it was funny, but Connie blinked back tears. It made me sick to see the fear and sadness in her eyes, but she might as well get used to it. The bottle is never far from him now. How much longer will I have the strength to endure this life I do not want yet do not know how to leave? How much longer will my daughters love an unresponsive mother?

In the distance I hear a ship's whistle. As dawn breaks, fog must be thick on the water. A Great Lakes freighter is signaling. The captain and crew will be safe. Sometimes I want to walk into the lake. Walk until my feet no longer feel the pebbles and sand beneath them. Walk until I swim. Then swim until my strength is gone and I become one with the beautiful aqua water. But like Connie's nightmare, what I want is only a dream. I close my eyes and turn towards the window. Daylight will soon signal time for us to rise and begin another day. Until then, I'll think of the fog and water and what could have been if only I had held my passion in check. If only I had fled before I stepped into the marital trap. If only Phil would stop boozing. If only Connie would tell me what's bothering her. If only. If only.

What Day Is It?

Ma and I are sitting across from each other in the living room. Her nose is buried deep within the folds of Sault Ste. Marie's only newspaper, *The Evening News*, and I'm knitting another winter scarf. Although we're not watching it, the television's blaring. "As the World Turns" is just signing off and a Canadian cooking show, "The Urban Peasant," is coming on. I glance at James Barber as he prepares another simple meal, something with onions, green peppers, garlic, and beans. I've been watching the man cook for three years, and I don't think he could do it without the help of onions, green peppers, and garlic. It's four o'clock on a crisp January afternoon. Ma peeks at me above the paper.

"What day is it?" she asks.

"It's still Thursday, Ma, just like it was five minutes ago when you asked."

"Thursday? The paper says Wednesday. The paper can't be wrong."

"That's yesterday's paper. Today is Thursday."

"Are you sure?"

"Yes."

"Then why does the paper say Wednesday?"

"Ma, today is Thursday. Take my word for it."

"Well, if you're sure."

Sure? I'm not sure about anything anymore. Sometimes I think she does this "what day is it" game on purpose. Sometimes I think she wants to take me with her into an unknown and fearful world, a place in her mind that builds its own reality. I don't know which is worse. Ma's losing battle with dementia or my losing battle with Ma. Sometimes I think she'll come back from that dark, internal place she drifted into last year. Sometimes I'm sure all it will take is the familiar smell of a walnut spice cake baking in the oven to rescue her.

I ignore the television and watch Ma as she reads and rereads yesterday's news. Every now and then she calls my attention to something she finds interesting, like Howard Snarles dying in Florida or twin calves being born on the Bartlett farm. Mind you, Mr. Snarles is a stranger to us and we have no idea who the Bartletts are, but Ma likes to keep me informed. We're two old ladies cloistered within an old house. If someone walked into the room, they'd think we were sisters, one with gray hair, and the other with white. Her face, like mine, is fairly free of lines and wrinkles. Her hair is curly by nature. My curls come from the hairdresser. Time has bent Ma shorter than her actual five feet. My back is straight, and I proudly claim my five feet, five inches. We're both thin and angular. She lifts her small white face and glances at me. Her glasses have slid down her nose.

"What day'd you say it is?"

"It's Thursday, Ma. Try to remember." She shakes her head in disbelief and returns to her reading.

"Can't be Thursday," she mumbles. "The paper says Wednesday."

I return to my knitting. Ma rarely believed me when I was young. Am I silly enough to think she'll start now that I'm 62? I drop the ball of red yarn in my lap and lean my head against the back of my chair. I feel so old and tired. Maybe I should give up and put her in a home, but I wouldn't put a dog in the only nursing home in our town. My hands grip the arms of my beige swivel chair. I rock in a slow rhythmic motion, back and forth, back and forth, willing the tension to leave my body. I close my eyes and see Ma in my mind's eye. She looks perfectly normal sitting contentedly in her plaid recliner, reading the paper.

Well, normal except for the wild getup she's wearing. Today it's the turquoise shirt with white stripes that's at least 15 years old, frayed at the cuffs and permanently filthy no matter how hard I scrub the stains. Its buttons are gone and safety pins hold it together, but she won't part with it. It's not like it has sentimental value. I bought it at a garage sale when I lived in Grosse Pointe. It belonged to some rich stranger. Ma's green polyester pants are a holdover from the 1970s. The elastic's gone at the waist so another large pin, the kind that would hold a baby's diaper in place, keeps them up. Her Keds are ancient and each big toe sticks its head out from a hole the size of a nickel. She has three new pairs of shoes in her closet and lots of nice outfits, but she won't wear them.

"The cats are dead. The guy down the road killed them." She starts to cry.

"No, Ma. The cats are fine."

"He always threatened to kill them. I knew we should have kept them inside last night." She shakes her head and reaches for a tissue.

She's got a little pile of them wadded up on the end table next to her chair.

"Ma, one cat is on the couch, one's in the bedroom, and Sweetie is sleeping on the chair next to you."

"It's no use lying to me."

"Have it your way."

She softly cries into the Kleenex. It's hopeless. I wish the neighbor would kill the cats. I'm sick of them. It's in and out all day and all night, too. Ma sleeps through the racket, but I jump every hour when one or the other scratches on my bedroom door. It wouldn't be so bad if they actually wanted out, but all they want to do is play. As soon as I awaken and open the door, whichever one was there runs behind the couch or underneath a chair where I can't reach it. If I go back to bed, the cat waits until I'm settled and then the game begins all over again. I'm half out of my mind from lack of sleep, but Ma doesn't see this. All she sees is that the cats must stay in so the neighbor won't kill them. I put them out before I go to bed, but she gets up and lets them in. Nights have become a nightmare. I'd gladly buy the neighbor a rifle and box of shells if I thought he's use them.

"I see in the paper where Bush is going to be President. I thought he was a few years ago."

"That was his father."

"Sort of like John Adams and John Quincy Adams. Let me see. George Washington, John Adams, Thomas Jefferson, James Madison, James Monroe, John Quincy Adams. Who comes next?"

"I have no idea, Ma."

"What do you mean? When I went to school we had to learn all the presidents. I knew them by heart. Now let me see. John Quincy Adams..."

I've heard this so often I could scream. Who cares who the presidents were? They're all dead. Even the live ones are no good, corrupt and immoral. If I could just get her interested in something to keep her mind active. She has no interest in jigsaw or crossword puzzles or anything else for that matter. She's outlived all her friends and enemies, too, right down to the last despised in-law.

"What day is it?"

"Thursday, Ma. Today is Thursday."

"You don't say?"

"Trust me, Ma. It's Thursday."

"That's right. We're out of the nineteens, right?"

"Yes. It's 2001 now."

"Is that a fact?"

"You know it is, Ma."

"Now why would you say a thing like that?"

"You've got to try to remember."

"I'm not crazy, you know."

"Then don't act like you are."

"Just wait until you get old."

I shudder when she says this. I get a cold shiver right up and down my spine. It's a curse she puts on me. I suppose God will punish me for my lack of patience, even lack of love sometimes in dealing with her, but heaven help me, I try my best. Never in my wildest dreams did I think I'd end up living with her, but there was no one else to help. I'm an old maid English teacher. I retired at 53, enjoyed two years of retirement, then the call came from her doctor that she couldn't live alone. I returned home from Grosse Pointe to do my duty. We had a good time during the first years. We'd go places and visit like the two old ladies we were. Losing her memory wasn't a gradual thing. It happened so quickly I didn't even notice it. It was like one day she was here and the next day there was a stranger living in her skin. I don't know who was more bewildered, she or I. She was puttering in the garage on a warm summer afternoon five years ago. When she came in she said something didn't feel right. She hasn't been the same since.

"What's that I hear?"

"I don't hear anything, Ma."

"Is it the wind?"

"There is no wind, Ma."

"Listen."

"I don't hear anything."

"I'm not imagining it."

"I just don't hear anything."

"I bet it's a cat trying to get in. Where's Scotty?"

"He's right there on the couch."

"I don't see him."

"Right there, Ma."

"You can tell me if he's dead too."

I put down my knitting and carry the cat to her. "See? He's right here."

"Well, you don't have to shout. I'm not deaf, you know. I can see he's right here."

I walk to the kitchen and start dinner.

"Don't bother fixing anything for me. I'm not hungry."

"I'm hungry, Ma." She prefers to eat alone. She's always been that way. I remember holidays when I was young. She'd wait on everyone and when the kitchen was empty, she'd settle down with her meal and enjoy it. Once I asked her why she didn't eat with the rest of us and she merely said it was more pleasant to eat by herself.

"Before I start dinner, Ma, how about I run a bath for you?"

"What for?"

"I just thought it might be a good idea."

"Are you telling me I stink?"

"No, Ma, but it has been a while."

"People wash too often. It's not healthy for the skin."

"A nice warm bath with bubbles. How's that sound?"

"Fine if you're three years old. I don't need a bath."

"But it'll relax you."

"I'm relaxed enough. Maybe you should have a bath."

"I'll lay out that new outfit you got for your birthday. The pretty blue one."

"I'm not taking a bath and I'm not putting on new clothes. What I have is good enough. Return the new clothes to the store and get your money back."

"I didn't buy it for you. Polly did. She'll be disappointed if I return it."

"Who the hell is Polly?"

"Don't swear, Ma. You remember Polly. She's the widow who lives across the street."

"I don't know any Polly. That's a bird's name."

"She tries to be your friend."

"I don't want a friend with a foolish name. She's probably an old busy-body who wants to poke her nose into my business."

"She's just being friendly and trying to help me."

"Help with what?"

"With you, Ma."

"But you don't help me. Why do you need help doing something you don't do? Does it take two people now-a-days to do nothing?"

"You don't understand."

"Quit making me out to be helpless. I can fend for myself. I don't need your help or that bird's either."

"I'll draw your bath."

"You can draw anything you want, but I'm staying put."

I give up. Bathing isn't going to happen, so I fry slices of meatloaf and warm up mashed potatoes and cooked carrots from yesterday. Ma sits at her place. I take the chair next to her. We eat our meal in silence and drink hot Lipton tea with our dessert. Suddenly, Ma smiles and tells me I'm a good cook. For a brief moment I forget her mind's drifting away from me. I get a warm feeling throughout my body. I'm a child again and Mama's going to keep me safe from all life's harms. She's going to read to me, listen to my troubles, and love me whether I'm pretty or not. I watch as she finishes her slice of apple pie. She puts down her fork and wipes the corners of her mouth with a paper napkin. She looks at me with those big, beautiful, trusting green eyes, eyes I always wished I had, but that now have a vacant look to them.

"That was very good," she says. "Very good, indeed."

"Thank you, Ma. I'm glad you enjoyed it."

"You sure know your way around a kitchen."

When the last dish is washed and put away and the kitchen is tidy, I return to my chair and pick up my knitting. I'm making a scarf for myself. Ma's chin is resting near her chest and she appears to be sleeping peacefully. Suddenly she jerks her head up and her eyes pop open. She looks lost.

"What day is it?" she yells.

"Today is Thursday, Ma. Thursday." She smiles, nods, and goes back to whatever corner of her mind she inhabits when she leaves me. I get out of my chair and walk towards her. I tuck the brown afghan underneath her chin. She sighs and pats my hand, her way of telling me she loves me. I kiss her forehead and return to my knitting. The room is quiet except for Scotty. His purr sounds like the Soo Line train crossing the trestle six miles away. It's his way of telling me all is well. And it is, really. It's only Ma's faulty memory that changed things, but I can live with that. I suppose I can even live with the cats pawing at my bedroom door in the middle of the night, awaking me from a deep sleep because they want to play. I can even live with today being Thursday or Wednesday or whatever day Ma wants it to be. What would be difficult to live without is my mother's love.

Aunt Betty's Secret

Whenever someone took a picture of Aunt Betty, she stuck out her tongue, raised her eyebrows, and opened her eyes as wide as possible. She looked like a fool in every photograph. When asked by the relatives in Detour Village why she insisted on acting so ridiculous, Aunt Betty merely smiled before sticking out her tongue and raising her eyebrows. She was a strange woman who had never married, never borne offspring according to legend, had very few friends, and never bothered anyone for anything. She was also much maligned by kinfolk who were waiting for her to die so they could divvy up her money and chattel.

Because she had worked all her life and saved every dime she had earned, Aunt Betty was rich. Like a lot of rich people, she was also a little on the stingy side. Mind you, she paid me—her housekeeper and companion—a fair wage for a fair day's work, so she wasn't stingy with me, only with the relatives who never looked her way until they wanted something. She would tell me that whenever any of them came to visit, especially the young nieces and nephews, they didn't visit at all. They came to complain about money problems. Some needed car repairs. Others needed vacations. Some required major dental or cosmetic work. The list of needs, wants, desires, and ailments was endless and regardless of the complaints, all expected Aunt Betty to fork over the cash.

A few summers ago in 1987, when Aunt Betty had reached the age of 91, a rather unappealing niece named Eleanor asked for $7,000. When Aunt Betty inquired why such a large sum was needed, Eleanor told her it was none of her business. Eleanor needed the money, get it out of the hope chest, and get a move on was her response. It was then Aunt Betty asked me to open the front door and if I felt so inclined to give Eleanor's arse a swift kick as she exited. Needless to say, I opened the door but refrained from the kick. After I finished vacuuming the living room carpet and washing the kitchen walls, Aunt Betty invited me to join her for a cup of tea. We had a good laugh at Eleanor's expense.

Betty insisted I call her "Aunt Betty." It drove the relatives crazy because so far as they knew, we were not kin. She didn't like people. It had taken her three years to warm up to me just like it takes time for a wart to sprout black hairs, but I was born with an easy-going nature and tended to ignore her insults regarding my lack of cleaning skills. When she found a crumb underneath the toaster, she hauled me away from scrubbing the floors to go over the counter again with a rag soaked in bleach. "Do things right the first time," she often said. "You accomplish more in a day when you don't have to go over what you've already done if you've done it right the first time." Aunt Betty enjoyed giving me little cleaning tests like hiding a bobby pin or paper clip underneath her bed to see if I would find it when I vacuumed. Or putting a piece of string behind the toilet tank. Or leaving her toothbrush on her nightstand. I always passed the tests, and although neither of us ever mentioned them, she would grin and tell me I was a treasure she couldn't do without. The implication was clear to us because we understood each other.

A few weeks ago, Aunt Betty received a letter from her German cousins whose home was in Scranton, PA and whom she had not seen since the family reunion 25 years ago. They invited themselves to visit her. This was a surprise as the only communication between them was a yearly Christmas card with a few words scribbled on it. They always assured her they were in the best of health, but their letter indicated they were not and wanted to see their beloved cousin one more time before they died. There were three of them—two men and their sister. They were 79 year-old-triplets whom Aunt Betty loathed. They were well aware of her feelings, but that didn't stop them from coming. The spinster was called Olga and had sticky fingers.

Oscar and Fritz had enormous feet they displayed by wearing sandals in warm weather. If there was one thing Aunt Betty despised, it was men in sandals. However, she responded to their letter and said they could come in July if they promised to pay their own way, book hotel rooms in Cedarville, take their meals at local restaurants, and stay no longer than two hours at her rambling home along the shoreline of Lake Huron. They could spend the rest of their time visiting other relatives. Two hours was all she was willing to give them. They agreed and early on the morning of July 12, I was sent to the airport in Kinross to pick them up. It was easy to spot the trio as they left the plane. They looked as close to triplets as two men and one woman can get. They all had white hair and wore black rimmed glasses. The men were dressed in black suits which looked ridiculous when paired with their bare feet in Birkenstock sandals. Olga wore a long black dress and sturdy black oxfords. An enormous black plastic purse hung from her arm. Each carried a black Samsonite Pullman suitcase. They had the appearance of Europeans who had just entered America and had no idea how they got here and even less idea why.

I called to them as they entered the small terminal and introduced myself as Aunt Betty's charlady, Scarlett "Blossom" Becker, and extended my hand which they gave a puny shake. I attempted to take their luggage, but they would not let go of it. We walked to Aunt Betty's 1969 Ford Fairlane and I opened the trunk. I had forgotten about the bags of top soil and cow manure I had purchased at Walmart yesterday. Luckily, there was enough room to lay the suitcases across the slightly damp bags. I held the passenger door open for Olga, but she said she preferred to ride in the back with her brothers. I was not going to argue. As I turned on I-75S, Olga asked if I always drove at a breakneck speed to which I replied if I didn't drive the minimum speed on the freeway, there was the possibility of a state police officer stopping and chastising me for driving too slow. Olga, Oscar, and Fritz grunted. I suggested they hold hands and pray for our safe arrival at Aunt Betty's.

Olga rummaged in her purse. I glanced in the rearview mirror as she handed each man a black rosary and kept one for herself. When they finished praying, they peppered me with questions. How was Cousin Betty's health? Did she have a gentleman friend? Where did she keep her cash and jewelry? Did she have a safety deposit box or a safe in her house and did I have a key or the combination? Who visited her? Did she sell her mink stole or the diamond engagement ring from the lovely man she was to marry until he was killed while climbing the Verdon Gorge in France? Had I seen that spectacular button bracelet from 1920 or the priceless one with diamonds? Where did she keep her income taxes?

I fielded the queries as best I could, reminding them I only cleaned for her, we never talked about her assets, and it might be a good idea if they saved their questions for their cousin. After that, we rode the next 50 miles in silence. They noted that it was a long drive and what a perfect name "Detour" was for the nondescript little village we were entering. The triplets had never been to the Upper Peninsula. From their many questions regarding the state of her health, it was obvious local relatives had hinted that dear Cousin Betty was about to kick the bucket.

When I pulled in the driveway, Aunt Betty was in the yard weeding her petunias. She didn't look up until I blasted the horn—one long, two shorts—just like a passing freighter might do. Her trademark red cotton bandana was wrapped around her white hair. She wore what she always wore—a pair of old plaid slacks, a paisley blouse, and a long sleeved ratty looking yellow-turned-brown cardigan sweater with the buttons missing.

"What took you so long?" she hollered. "I thought you were never coming." She walked to the car, took off her gloves, and shook hands with the cousins. "Do you want something to eat?" she asked. "There's yesterday's sauerkraut and wieners and brown bread from Sune's grocery. I can't guarantee how fresh the bread is but we all know sauerkraut never goes bad. Blossom bought the wieners from Neville's in the Soo, so they're excellent." Without waiting for a reply, Aunt Betty marched into the house, and we marched behind her. Instead of the dining room table being set, we sat at the table in the breakfast nook. Instead of her good Bavarian porcelain, she had laid out paper plates and plastic forks.

The yellow nook was small as was the table. The yellow straight-back chairs with rattan seats were uncomfortable. The pungent odor of sauerkraut permeated the tiny nook. The triplets each weighted a minimum of 250 pounds as did Aunt Betty. At 200, I'm also a large woman. The outdoor temperature had reached 89F degrees and the temperature inside was a close second. Olga said she felt quite faint. Aunt Betty dropped two ice cubes into her glass of water and suggested she take a good slug and calm down. Oscar asked if he might take off his jacket to which Aunt Betty said it was bad manners to disrobe during a meal. Fritz said nothing, but turned from white to pink to bright red. I was sure his face would end up in his plate at any moment. Aunt Betty ignored her company and consumed her meal with a great amount of lip-smacking and second helpings.

Finally the eating stopped because Aunt Betty laid down her fork and announced, "If you've come for my money, you're wasting your time. I'm leaving everything to Blossom." Looks of horror crossed the triplets' faces. Aunt Betty doubled over in laughter. She got up from the table and pointed to the door. "You might as well leave now as later," she said. "You won't change my mind no matter how much crying or threatening you do so there's no point in trying. My will is airtight. I'm on video tape with my lawyer on one side of me and my physician on the other so you're out of luck at contesting it. Your two hours are up."

The relatives protested, explaining they had no interest in her money or anything else, not even the beautiful Bavarian tea set staring at them from the dining room's china cabinet. Before the war to end all wars, Aunt Betty's parents had managed to smuggle the china out of Germany as well as some priceless gems. Olga said the trio had traveled coach all the way from Scranton just to visit her because they loved her, but it held no sway with their hostess. She marched them to the screen door, pushed it open, and waited while Olga, Fritz, and Oscar exited. It was my task to drive them to the motel nearest the airport. Aunt Betty insisted they leave in the morning on the 6:30 flight to Detroit where they would change planes and head home. On the way to the motel, no one spoke.

When I returned to Aunt Betty's, I found her slumped over her petunias. At first I thought she was inspecting for aphids. I was about to enter the house until I realized she wasn't moving. I called to her but there was no response. I rushed to her side and grasped her head in my hands. Her neck fell backward, her eyes stared into space, and I knew she was gone. The heart that had beaten so faithfully for so many years had finally given up. I left her as I found her and ran to the house. After calling 911, I returned to her side, stroked her hands, and waited for the ambulance. Once she was taken away, I phoned the hotel where the relatives were. However, the desk clerk informed me that a woman had picked them up. I figured it was Thel, a cousin through marriage who made a point of sticking her nose into Aunt Betty's business as well as her wallet. It took exactly one minute to make a decision. I would not notify the relatives that Aunt Betty was gone. They could find out she was dead by reading her obituary in the paper. I was sure Thel would send them a clipping.

Although I knew there was no point, I started the Fairlane and followed the ambulance to the hospital. Aunt Betty did not need the aid of a doctor. She needed an undertaker but out of love and respect, I did the right thing. Once she had been officially pronounced dead, I drove to Bailey-Newhouse Funeral Home in Sault Ste. Marie and made the necessary arrangements. Then I drove to the house I had shared with Aunt Betty since I was three years old. I looked at all her lovely trinkets and remembered where and when she had purchased each one. I touched her beautifully upholstered chintz chairs and the matching davenport. I gazed at the picture of her parents on the fireplace mantle. I touched every end table, every lamp, and every precious Hummel she had collected. I held the only photograph of her and her sweetheart taken before he decided to scale one more gorge before they wed. Then I sat on a yellow chair in the yellow breakfast nook and wept until my tears filled all the yellow napkins from the yellow holder.

I did not want Aunt Betty's money or her possessions. I wanted her. She had always made me feel safe. Yes, she was grumpy at times and many of her ways seemed odd, but she was good to me. She had rescued me from the Emma Nason orphans' home. She had saved me from a life of torment and poverty. She had treated me as her own. I was so lost in thought, I did not hear Thel and the triplets enter the house. I didn't even feel Thel's silk scarf around my neck until it was choking me. I had just enough time to see my attacker before I tumbled from the chair to the floor. I lie as still as death and listened as Thel and the cousins opened every drawer in the kitchen before moving to the dining and living rooms. They searched the china cabinet, overturned pieces of furniture, ripped the cushions, tore pictures off the walls, and cursed when they found nothing. I heard them stomp upstairs. I listened as the crash of Aunt Betty's belongings hit the floor. When they discovered her hope chest held nothing but winter blankets, I heard them curse her to the deepest depths of hell. Then they returned downstairs, grabbed the Hummels, slammed the front door and left.

When I felt strong enough to move, I phoned the funeral home and asked if they had notified Thel to which they said indeed they had. In a small village like Detour, everyone knows everyone and what they don't know, they make up. Apparently when the neighbor closest to our house saw the ambulance pull in our driveway, she called her friend, Thel, who called the hospital and then the mortuaries. Within minutes, Thel had learned Aunt Betty was gone. She immediately picked up the triplets and drove to our house with the goal of finding Aunt Betty's cash before the other relatives knew of her death and descended upon the house while everyone else was at the wake.

I tidied the house as best I could and made it presentable to neighbors who were stopping by and expressing their condolences. After the sun went down, I locked the front and back doors, ate a little sauerkraut, and sat in my chair, the one opposite Aunt Betty's. Then I reached for the photograph laying on the end table next to me. I carefully removed the glass. Thel had cracked it in her frantic search for money. Then I removed the cardboard back and untapped the key to Aunt Betty's safety deposit box at Central Savings Bank in the Soo. I smiled at Aunt Betty and her sweetheart as I held the photograph.

If anyone had been watching, they would have seen my tongue stick out, my eyebrows raise, and my eyes made as wide as possible as I silently thanked the woman I called Aunt Betty when we both knew perfectly well she was my mother. I brushed away a tear and took my birth certificate that had also been stored behind the picture of her and my father. I pressed my lips to both. Then I turned off the living room light and made ready for bed. In time, all would be exposed, but for tonight Aunt Betty's secret remained known only to me and my dear departed mother.

Misbegotten Larke Jones

Larke Jones looked at his reflection in the hall mirror of his 1968 Marlette mobile home and smiled. He liked what he saw—thick blonde hair falling in a sexy wave over his left eye, pork chop sideburns trimmed to a sharp point, yellow shirt open, exposing his golden chest hair. He turned up his collar. He liked it better that way. It gave him an air of authority, of independence and sexiness that no turned-down collar could match. He rolled up his shirt sleeves and adjusted his Wranglers that hung low on his thin hips. The jeans were threatening to drift too low and expose his bulge. He shifted it to the right, but the damn thing had a mind of its own and shifted back again.

He laughed as he thought of the two beauties waiting for him at the Cedarville pier. Left or right, it wouldn't matter once he got between them. Patsy or Gina would take charge of it, and they could dress it any direction they chose. He winked at himself as he turned to leave. He wouldn't bother to leave a light on. Dianne, his wife, wouldn't be home tonight, and he had a good feeling he wouldn't make it back either.

As he stepped outside something came over him. He couldn't call it guilt, exactly, but it must have been something like that because the excitement he had felt while getting showered and dressed left him as soon as the damp air from Lake Huron hit his face. He slid behind the wheel of his red Stingray, turned the key, blasted the radio, and with the top down, drove away from Lot 15 of the trailer park. He reached for the pint of Gordon's in the glove box. The vodka felt good as it traveled down his throat. It was a friendly, comfortable feeling, one he knew well and looked forward to each day. His carefree mood, his untouchable, impenetrable psychopathic self returned, and he was ready for the night. No guilty feelings for him. Live life to the fullest and forget about everything except booze and easy women.

He drove slowly down South Meridian Street. No point in getting harassed by the local cops. There'd be plenty of time to floor it once he was on I-75 heading north towards Sault Ste. Marie. He wanted a night of dancing and drinking at the Northview Lounge on Portage and some fun with one of the gals who had been begging for it all week. That's what Larke did best—bang the women. Sex was all he thought about. It was what he lived for—that warm moist hiding place between a woman's legs. He had his first lay when he was nine, but he had watched his stepfather hump his mother long before then. The first time he saw Virg on top of Ma and heard her grunts he had yelled at him to get off her. He ran to the bed and punched his tiny fists into Virg's back. Ma told Larke to leave the room. Her voice was cold and harsh. *Get out,* she had said, *get out and stay out.* Larke ran to his bedroom which was really a small pantry off the kitchen. He threw himself on his cot, buried his face in his pillow and cried, but as he grew older and understood what Virg was doing to Ma, he wanted to do the same to the neighborhood girls.

Larke headed towards the pier, but neither Patsy nor Gina was there, just a young couple holding hands and watching the sun set. He looked at them for a minute, looked at the way the woman leaned into the man and seemed to hang on his every word. He thought of Dianne, his bride of seven months. He wondered whom she was leaning into tonight, whose words she was hanging onto as she drank herself blind. She knew Larke had married her due to her father's influence. He didn't like her let alone love her. He was late for the wedding, still reeling drunk from the stag party the boys had given him and still smelling of sex from another woman. Dianne's brothers managed to pull him together and sober him up long enough to say the vows, but even as he walked down the aisle with Dianne on his arm, his eyes were checking out the guests, searching for a fresh lay. The couple was faithful to each for one week. After all, it was the age of free love and all that. He took another swig of the bottle and lit a Lucky Strike. He inhaled deeply, blew the smoke out through his nostrils, and watched as it floated away.

Larke worked hard all day. His buddy owned a construction company and threw odd jobs to him whenever he was sober enough to handle menial labor. Today he was sober and Bobby had gotten his money's worth from Larke. He was hired as a lackey at a building site in Detour, but no matter how demeaning, Larke could take whatever Bobby dished out. Beneath his yellow shirt, the muscles of Larke's arms were hard and strong. He was a tall man—over six feet—and every inch of him as sound and sleek as a Kentucky thoroughbred. When he ditched his shirt on the job, even men who were much stronger had to admire his body. Firm, virile, young. He oozed sex appeal, and women were drawn to him like nails to a magnet. Everyone appreciated his body, everyone except his wife. She laughed at his skinny legs and long slender feet. She said his hands were too small for a man. They didn't match the rest of his body, and he didn't know how to use them. She said his Johnson was too short and slim, that she never knew if he was in her or still playing around. Dianne cut him every chance she got. He banged her hard, but she was the type of woman who could eat a green apple or read an article in Redbook while a man tried his best to please her. When he finished, she asked what took him so long, rolled her back to him and serviced herself.

Everything had started out good. Dianne's old man liked Larke and hoped he would settle her down. He enticed Larke with the promise of a new trailer and was as good as his word. His wedding gifts were not cheap. There wasn't a toaster or iron, a set of pillowcases or a coffee pot among them. Her old man bought them the new trailer, the snazzy Vette, opened a bank account with $3,000 in it, and gave them a honeymoon in Vegas that included gambling money. Larke had grown up dirt poor and couldn't believe his good luck. Dianne had taken to him right away. Between her lust for him and her dad's desire to get her off the streets, they were married within two months of meeting. Larke was a hard drinker, but once the wedding ring was on his finger and the old man was supplying the booze, he drank even more. He enjoyed it. He wasn't like most fellows. He wasn't running away from anything. He had finished his three year stint in the Army and had even been lucky enough to avoid Vietnam and serve in Germany.

When he was discharged, his papers classified his rank as PFC, the same as when he completed basic training. So he didn't drink to escape the images of war or an unhappy past. At 24, he was too young to have much of a past. He drank because he wanted to, because the beer and booze made him more of a man, gave him the self-confidence and conversational skills he lacked when he was sober. He was funny when he was drunk. He was clever and quick-witted. He was the life of every party, right in the middle of the action where he wanted to be, where he needed to be. Women loved him. They loved his voice and the way he sang along with Elvis when the booze gave him courage. They loved the feel of his manhood next to them when he danced slow and held them close. Everybody—even Larke—loved Larke Jones when he had poured too much vodka down his throat.

The sun was gone now. The June night quickly lost the day's heat, and a shiver ran down his back. He didn't want to be alone tonight.

He better get a move on and find one of the girls before they picked up some other construction worker. He parked the Vette and walked into Anchor's Bar. The light was dim, and it took a few minutes for his eyes to adjust. Damn his left eye. It was the lazy one that wandered and made him look goofy. He'd been ashamed of it all his life. When he was little, Ma had dragged him to a doctor in Munising, and the quack told her Larke had to wear a black patch and exercise the eye every day or it would never get better. Ma believed him and paid for the bogus cure out of her meager wages as a housekeeper. She made Larke wear the patch every day for three months—all summer when he was seven. He was ashamed to leave the house, but Ma insisted he get fresh air. Kids laughed at him and called him names. His eye did improve, but only after there was enough money to buy proper glasses. When he was eight, he vowed nobody would ever laugh at him again. He would make others laugh at their own stupidity, and he would do it in such a way they would never guess he was mocking them. At the tender age of eight, Larke Jones was teaching himself how to become a psychopath.

Finally he could see through the haze of cigarette smoke. He leaned against the worn oak bar. "Vodka and grapefruit juice," he said to Mac who nodded and turned away. Gina moved through the crowd, claimed the stool next to him, ran her hand along his left thigh, let her fingers rest near his thing. He grew hard immediately. He turned and kissed her on the mouth, his tongue seeking hers, probing, sucking, demanding. She returned everything he gave and more. She'd been hungry for him since they were kids playing in the sandbox, showing each other their personals. She aborted his baby the summer he left for Germany, the summer of 1965, but she never told him. He wouldn't have married her. Gina was a lusty woman men loved to love, but they didn't marry. She knew that, but the knowing didn't stop the wanting, and the stolen time she spent with Larke was worth the sadness of losing his baby, seeing him go off to wherever the Army would send him, and then watching him return home and marry Dianne.

After many rounds of vodka, Larke was beginning to feel the booze. He liked the high. It made him feel in control. Gina was his for the taking. This bar was his. Mac was his. The music on the jukebox belonged to him. The bottles lined behind the bar were his. He had everything he needed within an arm's reach. He was king. Tonight was his night. He could do anything and everything. He had no past and no future. He only had now. Tonight he was the main player. The game belonged to him, played by his rules which never stayed the same for long. He was all-powerful, feigning a brilliance perpetually escaping him when he was sober and bound by his own ignorance. He was no longer a son, a brother, a husband. There was no memory of his stepfather's fist, then his belt, and when he still refused obedience, the dark closet he was locked into. There was no memory of that terrifying experience. It was gone, vanished like it had never happened.

There was no memory of the older brother who bullied him when Larke found out they were half-brothers, that he was a bastard and was only borrowing the Taylor name, waiting for the day when his true surname, Jones, was stuck on him. Larke had been an imposter, borrowing someone else's name much like a poor relation borrows a rich cousin's clothes with no intention of giving them back until suddenly and without warning, the demand for return comes. No, that memory of the Taylor name was gone, too, lost somewhere in the vodka. And the memory of his wife was gone as well. Dianne no longer existed. She was a flimsy vapor, a waif who floated in and out of his mind. She was something unreal and unwanted. He didn't need her anymore than he had needed the black eye patch, the cruel stepfather, the mean half-brother. He didn't need anyone. He didn't even need his father-in-law's payoff for making a would-be whore respectable by marrying her. The booze made him invincible.

Gina was whispering something in his ear. Larke threw back his head and laughed. He kissed her hard, pulling her tongue into his mouth until he bruised it. He had power over her, and he knew it. She was his one constant, like Ma. Why the hell did he think of Ma now? He was thinking of Gina, wasn't he? Ma liked Gina. They were the same—good, honest women. Ma was sober now and had been for years. He had finally forgiven her for looking the other way when his stepfather beat him. Ma had been weak, Larke knew that now, weak and drunk and just as confused as everybody else in his world.

"I've got to get out of here," he said to Gina or did he say it to himself or to Ma or Dianne? He threw some bills on the bar and waved to Mac. Gina's arm was around him, steering him towards the door, towards the pure night air. He wanted to get rid of her, to go home and find Dianne waiting for him, to start over again, to make everything right between them. Was he talking to himself or to Gina or were the words only swirling through his brain? Gina was lost in her own drunkenness. What did she know of loneliness and loss? What did she know of love? All his life Larke Jones had wanted one thing, but he couldn't quite put his finger on it, couldn't quite find the right words to shape it into being, to give a name to whatever it was he wanted. He wanted a nameless thing that would fill the void within him. Something that would calm his unspoken fears and make him whole. Something that would give form and substance to his life—an anchor—maybe. Yes, that was it. An anchor. Larke needed an anchor as strong as steel, hard, dependable, steady. Something that wouldn't cut and run when the going got rough as the going always did. But what was this anchor and did it even have a name? Was it an emotion he wanted? Or a safe place to rest? Was it a person? Was it God? Yes! Maybe that was it. It was God he wanted in his life, not the booze, not the easy women, not his mother, not his lost name, not Gina, not his wife. It was God.

Larke shook his head to clear it. He and Gina were in the Vette now. She was unscrewing a pint of Christian Brothers she had taken from her purse. The pungent smell of it brought him back from whatever precipice he had scaled. He was safe now as he felt the sharp bite of brandy burn his throat. He was on familiar ground. He took off his glasses and wiped his left eye with the back of his left hand. His wedding ring brushed his cheek. No matter. It was only a band of gold, a meaningless piece of jewelry. He turned the key. The Vette jumped to life, eager to be on the highway. The night was young. In the bar, he came close to facing something he couldn't name. Something that threatened to rip him apart and expose all the rejection, hurt, and loneliness piled inside of him like so much dry cordwood stacked in a shed. He wouldn't make that mistake again. He'd live life on his terms and his terms only. He was boss. His way or no way. Life was good as long as he shared it with a bottle and didn't do too much thinking.

He pressed hard on the accelerator, unmindful of cops that might be waiting to catch a Friday night drunk. He headed for the freeway. Janis Joplin scratched her way through the radio, her raspy voice a lifeline to anyone in need. Gina sang with her, and Larke joined in, "...take another little piece of my heart." He'd get through this night and the next and the next and all the tomorrows that awaited him. He was strong. He was free. Larke Jones was a man. This was the last thought running through his pickled brain as the Stingray jumped the median and landed in the southbound lane of I-75. The driver of the semi carrying a load of Canadian Club Rye in the Fruehauf trailer saw the red sports car as it flew through the air. He knew there was nothing he could do to avoid the collision. He felt guilty, but had he known Larke, he would have known this was the appropriate sendoff for Cedarville's favorite drunk. Misbegotten Larke Jones would have thanked the man for freeing him from his self-imposed prison. Joplin sang on, heedless of Larke as life slipped from his body and the void he had always felt was being filled by something more powerful and more beautiful than he ever could have imagined.

Junk Drawer Blues

For two years, Beverly had a love affair with a man who kept her in his kitchen junk drawer. Oh, not literally kept her there because they didn't live in the same state, let alone the same house, and Beverly was much too big to squeeze into anybody's junk drawer no matter how big the drawer and no matter how little junk there was in it. No, Beverly's sweetheart shrewdly kept her physical presence hidden from the people in his world in Salem, Illinois. To his friends, she simply did not exist whereas in Shingleton, Michigan where she lived, everyone who knew her knew she had a lover. It was her two years' worth of cards, letters, notes, presents, and old coins that Tony kept hidden in the drawer. Beverly made this discovery quite by chance.

During the Christmas holidays of 2001, Beverly visited her daughter, Olivia, in Louisville, Kentucky. When Christmas was over, Beverly thought it would be fun to visit Tony. He was only three hours away so she telephoned him early the morning of December 29. When her call went to his answering machine, she said she would see him soon. Then she hung up and kissed her daughter goodbye and drove to the Quick Mart on Hurstborne. She filled her Sable with gas, bought a large decaf coffee, and a glazed doughnut. She returned to her car, ate the doughnut, drank the coffee, and started thinking. She really wanted to see Tony but snow was falling, and she didn't want to drive in bad weather. However, if snow was falling in Louisville, it most certainly would be falling farther north so it made sense if she was going to run into snow anyway, she might as well head south. She put the car in gear and drove towards the freeway. Olivia had given her excellent directions. Beverly would have no trouble finding Salem. No trouble at all or so she thought. She was not a seasoned traveler and this was, in fact, the first solo trip of her entire life unless you count the seven hour drive from Detroit to Sault Ste. Marie which was only a straight shot up I-75N. She also had no experience or interest in reading a map. Olivia had printed one off the Internet. It was detailed and perfect in every way so it would be much easier to follow than a real map loaded with information she did not need.

Beverly wove through the Saturday morning traffic, which was no easy task, and merged onto I-64W towards New Albany/St Louis passing through IN then crossing into IL. Her map said she would travel 185.61 miles, so she settled back to enjoy the drive, knowing she was on the right road. Although snow was falling fairly fast and the road was slick in spots, she was glad to be going south. She knew Tony would be thrilled to see her. Well, thrilled might be too strong a word, but nevertheless, he would be happy. She tried to find something other than country music on the radio, but it was country or nothing. As she didn't like country, she inserted a tape she made for Tony but had decided against giving it to him. It contained some of her favorite songs, at least her favorite songs at the time she made the tape. Meatloaf's "Two out of Three" was blasting through the speakers, inviting Beverly to sing along, which she did while keeping her mind on her driving.

There were a number of accidents along I-64W. Obviously, Kentuckians were not used to driving on icy roads. Beverly managed to maintain control of her car as the Jeep in front of her crashed to a stop by plowing into the Dodge van in front of it, which narrowly missed the state police car. Actually, two state police cars on either side of the westbound lanes. Beverly wasn't sure if the three dogs running down the freeway had escaped from the upside down red Ford she passed or if the animals lived nearby and had caused the truck to flip in the first place. Either way, the dogs were unharmed and appeared to be having a race as they careened among cars in various stages of immobility. Luckily, Beverly was a fairly competent driver and managed to outrace the dogs. As she glanced in her rearview mirror, she noticed a pile-up of vehicles and hoped no one was hurt. She rewound "Two out of Three" and continued on her way.

About an hour into the drive, the weather was no better and the highway was worse. Beverly noticed another accident ahead of her and a line of vehicles waiting to enter the roadway so she took the next exit which happened to be the exact one she needed Exit I-57N towards Chicago for 12 miles before taking IL-161 Exit 109 towards Centralia 0.3 miles to IL-161 towards IL-37. This confused her because her map said it was a four hour drive to Salem and if this was the correct exit, she would arrive at her destination in less than three hours, or so she thought. Beverly pulled into the Mobile station off the exit, added two dollars worth of gas, and stood in line to pay. She thought it might be a good idea to ask the locals, who were discussing weather conditions and speculating on how long the snow would last, if she was heading in the right direction.

"Excuse me, but could tell me how to get to Salem?" she asked a young fellow with stringy blonde hair who was holding a cup of coffee he had just poured from the pot that rested next to the cappuccino machine.

"Salem?" he drawled. "Salem. Let me see. Hum. Don't rightly know, Ma'am. I's new 'round these parts."

Beverly thanked him and turned to three farmers who were discussing the pile-up on westbound I-64 that had been caused by a runaway tire bouncing madly across the freeway.

"Excuse me, gentlemen, but could you tell me if I'm on the right road to Salem?" she asked, feeling a bit like Dorothy in *The Wizard of Oz*.

"Salem? Well, let's see. If'n ya go out the frunt door an' make a sharp right, an' follow the road ya'll be on, it'll lead ya right ta Salem. It ain't fur."

"Hang on thair," his friend said. "That ain't right. She'd be better off ta..."

"Nay, yur both wrong. If'n she takes a right she ain't gonna find Salem that way unless she travels back ta cross over Spat's Landin' whair they dun tore up the road till..."

In total confusion, Beverly thanked Larry, Curly, and Moe, paid for her gasoline, and used the ladies room which was quite clean and smelled of cinnamon. Then she bought a bag of Pork Rinds with the change she found in the bottom of her purse and headed for her car. She tossed aside her Internet map and followed her new directions to the letter. She turned right where she was supposed to and then she turned left. Soon she would be in Tony's arms. The very thought made her heart beat a little faster and her lips break into a smile. She couldn't wait to see the look of surprise and delight on his handsome face.

Two hours later Beverly was still roaming through the countryside. The snow was gone, the scenery was beautiful, and the drive through Brown County National Forrest was exceptional. Such tall, dead trees. At least they looked dead or maybe it was just the type of tree they were—white trunks that looked for all the world as if one good gust of wind would bring them down on her vehicle. Beverly had a feeling that something was not quite right. All the highway signs she read had the abbreviation IN on them instead of IL, but, of course, she couldn't be in Indiana. She had left Kentucky and was in Illinois, wasn't she? Eventually, she saw a sign for Salem 35 miles ahead.

Tony had mentioned that Salem was a small, rural area surrounded by farms. Beverly had yet to see the farmland, but she was convinced the lonely looking horse she saw standing outside a broken down building was an introduction to the farms and rolling hills and meadows. However, they never materialized. Undaunted, she kept going, much like that pink bunny who hops around until his battery dies. The miles clicked by, as did the time. Beverly became less sure she was on the right road, less convinced that Salem was just around the next corner. After another hour of driving, she decided it was time to get new directions. She pulled into another Mobile station. Three females in various stages of womanhood from adolescence to menopause were looking at Playgirl as they stood behind the counter.

"Excuse me," Beverly said. "Could you please tell me what state I'm in?"

The trio looked at each other, stifling laughs. "Indiana," they answered in unison.

"I was afraid of that," Beverly answered. "I was looking for Salem, Illinois."

The tall, baby-faced teenager wrapped a strand of short pink hair around her index finger and said she'd never heard of Salem, Illinois, but Salem, Indiana was just a short piece down the road. She said it was a very nice town. Beverly thanked her, but said her business was in Salem, Illinois. The plump 30-something woman with curly brown hair said she'd never heard of Salem, Illinois. However, she was sure it existed because most states had a little town called Salem probably named after a town out east that had all the trouble with witches years ago when America was young and people with crazy religious notions were settling Massachusetts and all those other eastern states. Beverly thanked her for this bit of historical information.

Finally, the gray-haired matron told Beverly if she got back on I-69S for 77 miles and merged onto I-465S Exit 0 for another 26 miles then took I-70 Exit 9A-B towards Indianapolis/St. Louis for just a quick minute and then took I-70W Exit 9B on the left toward Terre Haute/St. Louis and followed I-70 for 135 miles she'd run right into I-57S towards Memphis to US-50 E/W Main Street via Exit 116 and she'd be in Salem, Illinois in about five hours. Beverly explained she had been on the wrong road over two hours, and wouldn't it be quicker to backtrack to the place where she'd made the wrong turn? No, the matron assured her. Going through Indianapolis was the best way to arrive in Southern Illinois. Beverly thanked the ladies for their help, got in her car, and drove away. She was almost in tears.

She wasted no time finding another gas station. She thought she'd give the Shell folks a try. First, she used their toilet, which was quite clean and had a nice pine scent to it. Then she asked the woman behind the counter, who had thin, wispy hair flying in all directions, how to get to Salem, Illinois. The woman's nametag said she was Patsy. Patsy was obviously in a world of her own, and said she'd never heard of any Salem other than the one down the road. She suggested Beverly purchase a Moon Pie and a cup of coffee to calm her nerves.

Just when Beverly was about to reach the end of her rope, a short, heavy-set woman wearing a black head scarf and a furry black jacket said she had heard of Salem, Illinois, and as soon as she paid for her gas she would lead Beverly through Elm Street and show her the entrance she needed to get back on the two lane highway she had traveled through Brown County that made all the necessary twists and turns to get back to where she wanted to go. Beverly hugged her and would have offered her five dollars, but she only had a ten spot in her wallet and felt foolish asking the clerk to cash it, which might make her look cheap as well as stupid. Beverly charged a *Universal Map Road Atlas* on her VISA, but as she had no idea how to read it and as her magnifying glass was at home on her desk, she never bothered to open it. However, she felt safer with the road guide settled on the passenger's seat next to her. It gave her a feeling of confidence, of *savoir-faire*, as if to say, "I, too, can read a map."

After a seven hour drive, Beverly did, indeed, find Salem, Illinois and Tony. He was busy working in the shop below his living quarters. He was helping the owners of the building, the Whit brothers, Ace and Duce, plane lumber for the ash rockers they made and sold all over Illinois and Kentucky and North Carolina and anywhere else they felt like driving. Tony gave a little start when he saw Beverly, as it was late in the afternoon and he figured she had driven home to Michigan. Although they had been lovers for two years, Beverly wasn't quite sure how she should greet Tony on his own turf, so she stuck out her right hand. Tony took it, wet his lips, pecked her on the cheek, and immediately told her to go upstairs, using the back staircase off the shop. Beverly left as quickly as she had come. She wondered why Tony hadn't introduced her to his friends, but no matter. She was here and he was here and that was all that mattered.

She let herself into Tony's apartment. It was neat and clean and very, very white. She walked over to the windows that looked out on the shop floor. Tony turned and waved. She watched the men for a few minutes. Tony was breathtakingly adorable in his brown coveralls, blue shirt, and brown boots. Then he turned his back to her, and she watched the men work together. They looked at ease with each other. She felt like an intruder, but no matter, she would wait for Tony to join her. When she was younger, she would have poked through his bureau drawers and cupboards and closets and desk and pockets looking for an indication of another woman, but Beverly had matured nicely and knew it was best to leave things alone. One never knew what one might find if one invaded someone's privacy. Why stir up trouble where there was none?

She sat on a kitchen chair, a pine spindle-back affair painted white. She felt a draft coming from the window, but that was okay because she was beginning to feel a hot flash spreading over her. She must remember to avoid St. John's Wort at all costs, even when only a trace of it appeared in herbal tea. Olivia had given her a variety box of Celestial Seasons teas for Christmas and before checking the ingredients, Beverly had downed a pot of tea before she realized that Wort was a main ingredient in the one she had chosen. The hot flashes would probably soon disappear. She hoped they wouldn't embarrass her in front of Tony. He was 56 to her 52 so he was no spring chicken either, but he could pass for 40 and rarely let a chance go by if he could tell someone, anyone—a hotel clerk, cashier, waitress, or a stranger on the street—how old he was and wait for them to *ooh* and *aah* over his youthful appearance.

After 30 minutes, Tony came up the stairs. Their relationship was a long distance one and they saw each other only once a month, as regular as Beverly's periods had been. She had no way of knowing that Tony was a neat freak to the point of obsession. He noticed a few specks of sawdust on the floor and mentioned that one of his buddies must have tracked them in earlier in the day. He left no doubt in Beverly's mind that what he really wanted was to tell her to wipe her shoes, or better yet, take them off before entering his apartment through the shop door where bits of sawdust could be tracked throughout his dwelling. Beverly immediately checked her footwear and scraped off microscopic flecks of sawdust adhering to the heels. She took a Kleenex from her purse and wrapped the offending specks in it. She hoped Tony hadn't noticed, not realizing that Tony noticed everything, everybody, every day.

They were awkward with each other. Beverly felt out of place. The apartment was immaculate, large, sparsely furnished, and absolutely stunning in its whiteness. The walls, the vinyl floors, the kitchen table and chairs, the appliances all gleamed before her. She thought of the tiny home she shared with her elderly mother. It was old, dark, and shabby and with three cats and a dog living in it, it was full of hair, dander, and carpet stains where the animals had either relieved themselves when no one was home to put them out, or had upchucked their dinners. Beverly knew Tony wouldn't last 15 minutes in her home, and she wasn't sure she'd last much longer than that in his spotless ice palace. He offered her boiled dinner his son had given him earlier in the day. Boiled dinner made by the hands of Tony's most current ex-wife. He had four of them all living in Salem and all still in love with him. Beverly politely declined. She mentioned she would like to get her car washed. The salt made it appear cream-colored instead of green. Tony looked horrified.

"Now?" he asked. Beverly said now would be fine unless he had other plans. She grabbed her purse and headed for the front door. She put both hands on the railing and walked down the long, steep flight of metal stairs that led to the parking lot where her car and Tony's truck were parked. He asked if she always made so much racket when she descended steps. Beverly hadn't noticed how hard she landed each foot on each step, but she agreed she was rather a loud walker for such a thin woman. She handed him her keys. "You drive," she said, taking no chances by asking for directions. Within a minute they were at the auto wash. Beverly handed him a roll of quarters and volunteered to help, but Tony said, no, he would do it. She noticed he didn't bother with the brush, but merely sprayed the car with water. When he finished, he pocketed the remaining quarters, slid behind the wheel and asked what she would like to eat. She said it didn't matter. She was hungry after her long drive and any place would do. She was looking forward to a good meal in a quiet restaurant, something intimate and cozy where she could tell Tony of her afternoon excursion into Indiana. She was sure they would laugh about her hopeless ability to follow directions. She settled back in her car and looked forward to a lovely dinner.

One can only imagine her surprise when Tony pulled into the drive thru of the local McDonald's.

"What'll it be," he asked, and regaining her composure, Beverly replied a garden salad, no dressing, would be fine. When the order was ready, he tossed the bag to her. Tony didn't want fast food. In all the months she had known him, not once had they eaten at a McDonald's or Burger King or Taco Bell. It was obvious, he wasn't about to start now. He would dine on the boiled dinner. At this point, Beverly learned something she had missed during Tony's brief visits. She learned he had no money. The meager living he earned from selling ash rockers didn't pay his bills. After he made a delivery to the store where Beverly worked, it was their custom to dine at the casino a few miles away in a town called Christmas. Although he paid for the meal, afterward he always asked for gambling money. He never wanted much, so she never questioned his request. If he won at the slots, he paid her back. If not, Beverly told him the $50 or $100 he owed her was a gift and repayment was not necessary.

She convinced herself it didn't matter that Tony was poor. She had driven all day for this rendezvous with the man she loved, and if Tony didn't have enough money to pay for a night out, well that was okay with her. She would enjoy the salad, thinking of all the calories a decent meal would have added to her slim hips. She would not think about his money problems. She would be happy snuggling next to him on his very clean sectional sofa, in his immaculate living room above a rocker factory. However, when they returned to his apartment, things didn't go quite as she had hoped. They ate in silence then Tony retired to his couch and Fox News and within five minutes he was fast asleep. For a few minutes, she watched him, watched his chest move as he breathed, watched his mouth open slightly, watched as the man she dreamed about dreamed his own dreams as spittle escaped his mouth and ran down his chin. Eventually he awoke, glanced her way, and told her she could sleep in his bed while he stayed on the couch. She nodded and headed for the bedroom.

When day broke on December 30, Beverly had already removed the sheets from the queen sized bed so Tony could launder them. She had showered, dressed, and packed, not that she had unpacked all that much. She wanted to peck Tony on his cheek as he slept in his pristine living room, but she was concerned she might awaken and startle him. Instead, she gave one last look around his beautiful, sterile living quarters and left him as he was. She quietly opened the door, glided down the metal steps, and unlocked her car. The morning was crisp and clear but very cold and water had frozen on the windshield. She turned on the ignition and fan, allowing the car to warm up as she scraped ice off the windows.

She was wearing her green Northern Michigan University sweatshirt with a yellow turtleneck underneath it. She had no need of her black jacket which remained in a heap on the back seat where she had tossed it yesterday or was that a lifetime ago? As she slid behind the wheel, she took one last look at Tony's apartment. He wasn't standing at the window. He was still snoring on the couch where she'd left him. She put the car in reverse, backed up, and let her eyes take in the building where Tony lived, burning it into her memory. Then she eased onto north Broadway. US-50N wasn't far down the street. She'd have no trouble finding it, no trouble at all, and she figured once she was well away from Salem, Illinois she would stop for a delicious breakfast and call Olivia who would guide Beverly safely back to Shingleton, back to the welcomingly old home located on a few acres just to the north of M-28, and to the loving old mother anxiously waiting her return.

It wasn't the fact of his poverty that bothered Beverly. It wasn't the McDonald's outing or the lack of introduction to the Whit brothers. It wasn't his obsession with immaculate living quarters. It wasn't his absence of affection or tenderness towards her. It wasn't even knowing she was a stranger in Tony's Salem life. Beverly was a mature woman who understood the need for discretion in a small town where his ex-wives lived and worked and where his son visited when he came home from college thinking his parents were still married after nine years of divorce. She could easily accept all that. No, what made Beverly decide to leave shortly after her arrival was something else entirely.

It was Tony's junk drawer that did Beverly in. When they returned from McDonald's, she had asked where he had hung the pewter fish chime she had given him as a birthday present. He told her it was in the kitchen drawer. When she asked about the metal Easter basket with the little bunnies in it he, again, mentioned the drawer. When she inquired as to the location of the NMU key chain and the laptop case and the history books and the 1945 calendar and the Mickey Mouse letter opener and the silver business cardholder and the business cards, he pointed to the junk drawer. Her letters, cards, and notes, so painstakingly written, were of course, in there as well. Beverly swallowed her anger and looked at the stranger she had fallen in love with at first sight one dry August day. She saw him clearly for the first time.

"You've kept me in the junk drawer for two years?" she calmly asked.

"Oh, no, no, of course not," he quickly responded. "I wouldn't dream of keeping you in a junk drawer. As I said. It's the kitchen drawer." He pulled open the biggest drawer beneath the counter. "See," he said proudly. "It's all there." Then he slammed the drawer shut and asked Beverly what she wanted to watch on TV and would she mind terribly if they watched Fox news?

Beverly had smiled. "I don't mind at all," she said. "Not one little bit." When he turned away, she took the Kleenex from her purse and scattered tiny bits of sawdust on the shiny white kitchen floor. "You just pretend I'm not even here," she said as she headed for the bedroom scattering sawdust behind her.

Three hours after she returned home, Beverly's phone rang. She let the answering machine get it. Tony said he missed her and couldn't wait to see her again when he drove north in a couple weeks. That afternoon she sent him a note. "Keep me in the junk drawer," she wrote on an immaculate sheet of white paper that she stuffed into a perfectly white envelope. Thus, with the stroke of a white pen, she ended her perfectly pristine, perfectly sterile two year, perfectly one-sided love affair.

Mary Beth Biggins and Her Beanies

Mary Beth Biggins of Trout Lake loved Beanie Babies and why wouldn't she? It was a Beanie Baby that had pulled her out of the muck and mire of loneliness and depression and back to the land of the living. She was ready to call it quits when she chanced upon her first Beanie. His name was Bongo. He was a sad looking little fellow with button-like eyes. She knew he was sad because it was an emotion she was well acquainted with. One look at him and Mary Beth was hooked. Here was a little orphan who looked sadder than she felt. Here was a nonjudgmental friend in need of a good home and tender affection. Not only did she buy Bongo, she also bought four of his brothers, all identical, all eager for love. When she got home, she put them on her kitchen windowsill. Each morning they greeted her and gave her a reason to face the new day.

Her life that had been so dull and monotonous suddenly became exciting. Mary Beth now had purpose and direction. The blood that had run so slowly, so listlessly throughout her ample body now surged and ran redder. It was almost as if she had taken on someone else's blood so drastic was the change. If she had been blessed with friends, they surely would have noticed the change in her appearance, but she was a loner and thus spared the embarrassment of having to explain the rosy color in her cheeks and the bounce in her step. She no longer wondered how to kill the day. It zoomed by all too fast as she drove from store to store in the Upper Peninsula searching for the latest Beanie. Hours that had once dragged endlessly by now whizzed. She was afraid her time would be all used up before she amassed an entire collection because Mr. Ty kept birthing Babies much faster than she could find them.

Mary Beth met the most interesting people when she drove to Sault Ste. Marie and waited in line to make her purchase at the Whitefish Bay Unfinished Furniture Store. There was Nancy, the heavy smoker from Negaunee, who was moving to California as soon as her Workman's Comp claim came through. There was Babs, the grandmother from Goetzville, who despised her grandchildren but felt duty bound to buy them gifts when there was no special occasion just to divert attention from her hatred. There was Joe, the retired Walmart greeter, who had sore feet. There was Lizzy, the Kinross divorcee who lived in her car. There were the twins, Dolly and Molly, two Stalwart spinsters who papered their rooms with $50.00 bills and told their relatives they were leaving all their money to the Beanies. There was the lawyer from Drummond Island who drew up the spinsters' wills and stood in line with them on rainy days. He held their umbrellas, hoping this little gesture would cement him a place in their memory as well as their wills.

Then there was Will, a handsome Finn from Engadine whose best friend had been crushed by a UPS truck when it backed over him as he tried to steal a box of Beanies. There was Dollar Settlement Calvin, a funny little man who wore long sleeved white sweaters over black ski pants throughout the winter and summer. There was Carla, the Eckerman welfare mother with her three children tugging at her sleeves and hoping she wouldn't leave them like their daddy had. And then there was Braid from Brimley. She was the one the others avoided for when Braid was around, trouble wasn't far behind. She was a pit boss at one of the local casinos. She had a tendency to turn violent if she wasn't first in line and, of course, she couldn't be first in line in every line in every town throughout the Upper Peninsula, at least not until she cloned herself. Wherever Braid was, the cops were nearby. If they didn't actually arrest her for assault, they at least warned her to go home and take her temper with her.

Mary Beth embraced them all. She never criticized, never offered an opinion, and never complained. If shopkeepers made the regulars stand outside the door while clerks unpacked boxes of Beanies, well, so be it. If there was a blizzard she simply wore a long skirt and a heavy woolen coat that was longer than her skirt. If the sun threatened to melt her, she kept her hands wrapped around the block of dry ice she took from her freezer when the weatherman said the day would be hot and humid. If hail appeared, she placed her handbag over her head. If the wind was strong, she made sure she stood by a stout man, a fellow who wouldn't mind her grasping his arm or leg if she felt the wind begin to carry her away. For the first time in her life, Mary Beth had friends if only for the duration of the wait in line. She became involved in their troubles, cried when a favorite pet died, rejoiced when a maiden daughter finally married, and congratulated someone who had good luck at the casino. The regulars knew each other's names, knew their habits, and knew how much money they had in the bank. Some resented the ones who had an inexhaustible supply of funds. Mary Beth was jealous of none and loved everyone.

Soon she became the most popular person in line. The younger women sought her advice on sick children and wayward husbands. The older people told her of their diseases and operations. The men complained about their wives. The wives complained about their husbands. Mary Beth returned home and shared the latest news with the Bongo brothers. There were so many people with interesting, intriguing lives, and all so eager to share their stories with her. For the first time in her solitary life, she didn't have to rely on her television for tragedies or comedies. She heard them first hand from the lovely people who surrounded her.

Mary Beth was not a pretty woman. She had no defining physical traits that would cause anyone to remember her except for her goatee. As goatees go, it was smaller than most, the whiskers of which stood out like bristles on a boar's back. Her gray hair was straight at the sides, cropped short at the bangs, and curled at the back, giving the illusion of three different hairstyles. However ridiculous that sounds, it suited Mary Beth. Her face was long. Her eyes were small and dark. Her teeth fit nicely in her mouth and when she wore them her smile was pleasant. She had a tiny chin that disappeared into her neck that disappeared into her shoulders. Her body had that roly-poly look many middle-aged bodies have when they've consumed too many Big Macs and ice cream sundaes.

Black had once been the only color in her wardrobe, but now she dressed in green like Erin or red, yellow, and brown like Gobbles, or white like Angel. Her sewing machine had stood silent for years but now hummed as she sewed outfits that would have made Edith Head spin in her grave, but no matter. Mary Beth was happy. Strangers who saw her walking down supermarket aisles or praying in church pews approached her as if they knew her. They inquired where she purchased her costumes and were thrilled when she said the designs were her own. They promptly asked her to sew for them. Mary Beth never turned down a request. Strangers became friends and were invited to her home where she took measurements and set to work. She cut, sewed, and pressed until a lovely dress, skirt, blouse, or pair of trousers emerged from various pieces of fabric. The colors were influenced by the Beanies, but the finished garments were from her imagination.

Soon, and with no advertising on her part, Mary Beth had a flourishing business. Her fame reached the ears of Mr. Ty. He considered bringing a lawsuit against her but changed his mind. Instead, he sent a congratulatory note and offered her a job as a designer. About the same time, she met Obby, a new clerk in the what-not store in McMillan. He was smitten the moment he saw her. Although it was against store policy, Obby faithfully tucked new Beanies in a bag, hid them on a shelf underneath the cash register, and saved them for Mary Beth. He never knew which ones she had purchased at other stores and he didn't care. He was anxious to please this fascinating woman. Obby's world was as lonely and isolated as Mary Beth's had once been. When his boss was around, it was impossible to hide his stash. Mr. Crane was a highly ethical man who refused to allow his employees to play favorites with the customers. At these times, Obby pretended they were his Beanies and put them in the back room. He waited until the coast was clear and then he called Mary Beth. Being a fellow of high morals himself, Obby did not give her his employee discount but sold the Babies at the regular price thus making Mr. Crane a tidy profit of $1.05 on each sale.

Mary Beth told Obby of the note from Mr. Ty, but also told him she would decline his request. Collecting Beanies and designing colorful clothes for strangers were nice hobbies, but her real passion was writing songs. Obby's ears perked up. Right in the middle of a sale he asked her to sing. She belted out a few bars of her own little ditties, unique and quite remarkable. Customers applauded. Obby told her he loved to pluck melodies on his banjo, but had no lyrics to accompany his compositions. He thought her songs would be a perfect match. Then he made the bravest decision of his life. He invited Mary Beth to dinner. To his astonishment and delight, she immediately accepted. When they met at Pizza Palace that evening, she brought her portfolio, opened it, and out tumbled hundreds of songs, all originals, all just waiting for the right music.

Obby couldn't believe his luck. He looked at the woman facing him and saw only her beauty, not the plain, long face, the goatee, or the ridiculous costume she wore. He reached for her hand, so soft and delicate in his own soft, delicate one. On her part, Mary Beth didn't see the short skinny wimp with the pockmarked face and thick eyeglasses. She only saw the adoration in his pale eyes, so she didn't hesitate when he asked her to be his wife. They wed the next week before the only Justice of the Peace in Chippewa County—a disgraced preacher who had lost his faith during a night of passion with a woman who wasn't his wife. They were happy to find him because Obby was an atheist and Mary Beth was between churches. When her Beanie friends heard the good news, they threw the newlyweds a party. Every Beanie Baby collector in Chippewa, Mackinac, and Luce counties attended the festivities.

Obby strummed his banjo, Mary Beth sang her songs, and everyone danced. Mr. Ty attended the celebration and gave the couple a generous check with which they purchased a 1999 Chevy Astro van. Mary Beth sold her cottage business to the non-believing preacher who had to make a living now that his congregation had kicked him out. One of the guests had invited a friend who was an agent and lived in Nashville. After hearing the talented middle-aged twosome, he signed them to a recording contract. When the party was over, Obby and Mary Beth packed their new van, drove to Nashville, and began recording the most successful CDs anyone had ever heard. They were an immediate hit with old and young alike and became regular guests on Oprah's show as well as David Letterman's and Jay Leno's.

Money was plentiful and life was good, but neither forgot they owed all their success and happiness to a sad looking Beanie Baby named Bongo. When they toured, Bongo and his brothers went with them. All the other Babies stayed home, stuffed into an oak curio cabinet purchased from the store where Obby had met the love of his life. As the years passed, the only recognizable thing about Mary Beth was her little goatee which she steadfastly refused to remove. It was a reminder of her former life when people shunned her as the crazy lady who lived alone and wore only black. It also kept vanity at bay. When Obby and Mary Beth decided they'd had enough of stardom, they returned to her little cottage in Trout Lake. The Bongo brothers were placed back on the kitchen windowsill. Every morning their adoptive parents told them all the latest news. As usual, they never said a word but never missed one either.

The fame of Obby and Mary Beth passed happily into oblivion as did the Beanie Baby craze. She often recalled a line from her favorite author, Thomas Hardy, who wrote in *Tess of the D'Urbervilles*, "It was as if they had never been and one day would be grassed down and forgotten." Mary Beth didn't care about being forgotten, but she hoped the "grassing down" business would be a long way off. Although they didn't speak, she was certain that Bongo and his

An Evening at Lucky's Tavern

One long albino hand rested on the bar, the other stroked the tall glass in front of her, moisture cooling her fingers. She picked up her drink and moved to a back booth, one she always shared with any number of causal friends. They made room for her and voiced their welcomed, but she only nodded. It was crowded, this little place called Lucky's in St. Ignace, a short drive east of where she lived in Moran. She turned away from her friends and watched the mating gestures of fellow voyeurs. When she turned back, she noticed how the candlelight cast images on the wall and exposed the imitation brick that was torn and peeling away. The last of her money lay neatly folded next to her hand, and she motioned Lucky for another beer. With nothing, neither fear nor courage nor anger nor anything as unreliable as love in her being, her psyche drifted in the night, a cluster of indiscriminate genes floating among the crowd.

Her name was Gloria. She had chosen it herself "to go with the way I look" she once explained. She was not tall, but rather that height some women reach when a certain attitude or situation lends an illusion of stature beyond their natural growth. Her long dark brown hair encircled her slender neck meeting in a "V" at her throat. Her forehead, partially hidden behind her bangs, was clear, free from lines as was her entire face, but at 33 one hardly expected a Mondrian mosaic. You noticed the eyes next. Those tiny colorless specks lost amid blue shadow. You couldn't call them honest eyes, but to call them dishonest was not fair either. They superseded both, adjusting to the demands of the people and circumstances around her. One thing you saw right off was the way they remained half-closed, and if you spoke to her and you were not a male, they closed even more, drawing into themselves, into her. Maybe not dishonest eyes, but certainly not eyes you would trust.

A thin pink ribbon comprised her lips, and her mouth housed perfectly white teeth. Her smile was wide if you were a man, sinister if not, but always given freely, quickly, as if the pleasure of meeting you was unparalleled by anything past or yet to come. Her head thrown back, teeth gleaming, brown curls shaking, pink mouth laughing was a sight not unlike those seen at carnivals or mime shows where everything is fantasy. She fooled you well, making you simultaneously repulsed and excited, and you wanted more. Friday nights always found her at Lucky's. Sometimes she grabbed the mike and whispered inaudible words through it, forcing a strange quiet to fall on the room. They all knew her, all the regulars at least, all the ones who were important and most of them liked her. When she had enough, she returned to her table and started on the shots lined there, drinking slowly, consuming each one, those elastic lips smiling a pink thank you to her benefactors.

Christian approached her as was his custom when alcohol took over. Once they had been lovers, and the child she severed from her was his. He had never forgiven Gloria for making the choice without his knowledge. He found company, solace in the bottle and an odd contentment, peace in Lucky's dim, nonjudgmental corners. He was a bum, a loser, a man void of hope, and he approached Gloria as if she were a queen.

"Got a gig today," he said taking the seat opposite her. "A real good one. Pay's good, hour's good." His dark hair fell over one non-descript hazel eye. His long jaw set sharply. He leaned into her, taking her slim, white hand in his large, tanned one, folding it into his arm. He felt her shrink from his touch, but he wouldn't release his grip, believing she owed him that much, believing that once a man and woman had mated they belonged to each other for life. Silly, romantic fool, dreaming angel dust dreams even when he wasn't high and thinking that just by thinking something was once so, he could make it so again and it would stay that way forever.

Gloria disengaged her hand and returned to stroking her glass. "That's nice," she said, knowing there was no need to say anything more, knowing that he knew that she knew that he was lying. There never was a job, although every Friday he told her of a new one and she responded in kind. She looked past him, above his head off into the blue smoke, her eyes following some transient path leading nowhere and everywhere and then she looked back at him, at the handsome face, full lips, scant beard and wondered how she had ever loved him. He was nothing, nothing at all. Not a man, not an existence, not a tangible glow like the candlelight. He sat quietly waiting for her love much as a dog waits for a pat on the head from its master. Gloria wanted to slap him.

She said nothing. She watched two couples walk in, the girls in office dresses, the men in blue serge suits, much too hot for May. St. Ignace lawyers, maybe, out with their secretaries, having told their wives they were working late. They took the table next to her booth. Gloria listened as they giggled back and forth in the ancient ritual of foreplay. They were disgusting. The girls—young and stupid, thinking they were special because they had been chosen by men much older and more pathetic than they—looked at the men with hopeful expectation. Fools, four fools Gloria thought. Their voices grated her nerves. Their empty, meaningless chatter made her stomach cringe as images from her past propelled her next to them. She was their age, now, sitting next to her boss, a lawyer from a respected Soo firm, and she was pregnant with expectation. What fools we women are. How little we change even as the 1970s Women's Lib pretense of change rages around us.

"The nights are long," Christian said. "You haunt them." His eyes had taken on a drunken blur, and Gloria could not stop him. Now he would lecture, telling her how immature, how foolish she was, telling her she needed him and why didn't she admit it. Her anger only increased as his look pierced her eyes, her soul, and he professed love, sanctity, unending, unconditional tenderness. She silently screamed, clawed his eyes, pounded his tall frame, made bloody his lips. Get away, she inwardly shrieked, leave me alone, get away, but she did not move her lips, and he—stupid, moronic, dull-witted creature that he was—he did not fathom the depths of her wrath. If his feeble, childish mind could have grasped her emotions, he would have evaporated at the strength of her loathing.

"I love you," he said, and this time not only did she look above his head, she also willed herself to look above her surroundings. Her mind floated out of Lucky's, away from the crowd, the jukebox, the noise and forced merriment, from the men in blue suits inching their octopus hands upward towards their secretaries' thighs. Gloria moved past the tables, past the candlelight, past the cigarette smoke, past the smooth bar, moved into the black night. At last, at last, she thought, I am whole.

She felt a spray of mist toy with her face, which was no longer her face, but the face of countless other women all searching for something they had long ago lost or had never had to begin with except in their imaginations. I am complete, she said, playing with the dark, slipping her hand in and out of it, chasing the ectoplasm of those who had gone before her and those who had never been. From a distance, she heard Christian's voice more desperate than she had ever heard it before, more pleading, more contemptible, "I love you," and this time, lost in her own being, consumed by her own lust of self, she responded, "Yes, yes, I love you, too." As the words slipped out, as she gave shape and form to them, they reverberated in her ears above the din of Lucky's. Christian reached for her hand and pulled her back to the bar. He shouldn't have done that. He should have left the words hang between them as hope for another day.

Gloria's voice became ice. "Get away," she said. "Get away," and the look of adoration left both faces. His crumpled in a drunken contortion of disbelief, and the look of madness spreading over hers strengthened so that you were enchanted by it and watched the elastic pink mouth stretch into a full smile coming to rest not on him, but on the amber of Hennessy he had discarded. She lifted the glass, thrust back her head, and swilled the cognac. "To us," she said. "To us and the child who never made it. Long life to us." She downed the drink in one gulp, and the look of madness softened, dissipated, went back into the night. I am not losing control, she thought. This night will end and tomorrow will be here, and all will be forgotten as everything is forgotten given enough time. You noticed her damp hair sticking to her temples, and how Christian's body lost itself in the booth. Without moving a muscle, you felt him get up, walk away, and disappear into the smoky haze as if he had never existed.

"Last call," Lucky yelled. "Last call." Gloria motioned for one more beer, and her eyes were not slits when she smiled the waiter a thank you. The candlelight played with the peeling brick, chasing it around the booth, jumping in and out of her glass. The albino hand almost caught it once, but when she opened her fist, it was empty.

The Orange Room

It was that time of evening on Sugar Island when the orange creeps into rooms, lending them a feeling of warmth and safety. Thirty-nine year old Victoria watched as rays of the setting sun filtered through her white curtains and spilled over her handmade rug. In the twilight, it didn't look old and tattered. She pulled it to one side and straightened it, then claimed the rocker built by an uncle who had died long before she was born. As she rocked, the day faded, but not before filling every inch of the room with a soft orange glow. She hugged herself with her strong, thin arms. It's not so bad being alone, she thought. Not when I have this orange room on a lovely quiet summer evening. It's not so bad.

And it wasn't, not really. Victoria had the silent room. She had the faded rug and the old-fashioned horse hair furniture and the oak rocker. She had the pictures that had once hung on her mother's walls now gracing her own. The same enchanting eyes that watched Victoria grow into womanhood now watched her four-year-old daughter grow through childhood. There was continuity, a common thread that held the room together, that carried over and lent itself to her so even when she was alone, she was not really alone, for the child she had been was still in her, and her own child, asleep in her pretty bedroom upstairs, was with her. Even the father Victoria had buried this morning was still there, albeit trapped behind a picture frame, and the mother who had died years ago and who perpetually grieved for all of them when she was alive, she, too, was there, smiling benevolently from her glass prison, free from all her worries.

The orange glow was almost gone now. Victoria looked out the double French doors and watched the sun evaporate from the sky. Flowers prospered around her white porch, and she breathed deeply of the sweet alyssum drifting their perfume through her open windows. She wanted to hold within the circle of her arms all the good things of the earth, all the memories in her heart, all the sweetness of her sleeping child. Just a moment longer, she thought. Just a moment longer let the twilight stay. She squinted into the gathering dusk, searching the shadows, the trees, the grass, the roses, the cosmos, even the incoming fog, searching for an answer to a question that wasn't a question at all, but an acknowledgement of her existence: Who am I and why am I here? The sun did not respond as it slipped away, and the fog did not answer as it shrouded the trees and flowers and earth in great gray patches. The grass, heavy with dew, did not murmur. The owl perched atop the barn made no sound.

As Victoria watched the sun bow and the orange fade from the room, her attention turned to a figure walking down the lane leading to her front door. The image was that of an elderly man. He walked slowly as if picking his way through a field of thistles or poison ivy or live mines. When he was almost to the porch, he stopped. He didn't seem like a stranger, and Victoria felt no fear. He seemed to belong to the house. To be part of it in some way. Maybe he had lived there long ago. Maybe he had built the dwelling and was returning for a visit. She would welcome the company on this peaceful July night. She smiled as she watched him mount the first step, then the second. When his foot was on the third, he hesitated. She switched on the outdoor light, flooding him in a warm yellow glow. He wore a white shirt and white pants. His hair was a mass of white cotton. As he moved closer, Victoria saw his face. It was lined and cracked as if he had weathered many storms on one of the Great Lakes or perhaps even the Atlantic.

"Come in," she said. "Come in. You are welcome," but there was no reply. He smiled and turned away, disappearing into the night. Victoria wanted to run after him—to run down the lane and catch him and hug him, but she returned to her rocker. A surge of loneliness swept over her. Perhaps the gentleman was alone and lonely, too, she thought. Then she was ashamed, for there was no way to tell if he was lonely or even if he was real or merely a vapor created by the fog. She admonished herself for transferring her feelings to him. He was an aged man, probably double her years, and whatever anguish there might have been, had most like been forgotten or replaced by the ills of old age. She roused herself, turned on some lights, and stepped into the night air as if she had just awakened from a dream.

She felt a rush of freedom as her bare feet touched the wet grass. She felt the cool misty fog enter her pores and renew her. She hugged herself and in that brief, spontaneous act, nothing mattered. Not the loneliness, not the fear of raising her child alone, not the search for an identity, not the stranger who vaporized, not even the death of her father could touch her. Songs sprang to her lips, and she softly sang the lullabies her father had sung to her. She saw him now as he appeared before her—a strong, plain man, a good man. She felt his strong arms around her. She was dancing with him, and it didn't matter that he no longer walked among the living, for he walked with her in her heart and that was enough. The glorious evening, the beautiful dark held no fear, no mystery, and she danced and sang until she laughed and wept and laughed again and became one with the night. She was wet and cold and that didn't matter, either, for this was summer, and it was okay to be wet and cold and happy and sad. She knew her arms were empty now, that whatever apparition had sought her out was gone, but that was okay, too. Eventually Victoria ran toward the light pouring from her living room.

She did not close the drapes but returned to her rocker and wrapped herself into a warm patchwork quilt. Her ponytail had come loose, and her hair clung to her neck. She pushed it away. In the distance she heard the growl of a foghorn as one of the freighters passed through the Soo locks. She thought of the sailors on the boat, thought of the father of her child as he worked his shift in the engine room of the *Tregurtha*. She wondered if he thought of her and his child. Probably not was the only honest answer. Probably not or he would be here with us. He would have taken leave to stand by Victoria as she watched her father's coffin being lowered into the ground.

As she climbed the stairs leading to her daughter's bedroom, she forced any sad thoughts from her mind. People were the way they were. You had to accept that. People were genetically programmed long before they were born. Their DNA was unalterable. Hoping and praying people would change was an exercise in futility. Victoria entered Alana's room. The little one had rearranged herself in her bed and was sleeping peacefully. Victoria looked at the child she had created. She touched the little hands and marveled at their softness. With her right index finger, she gently outlined Alana's delicate, beautiful face. Victoria breathed the pure clean essence of her daughter. The little girl sighed. "Mama," she said. A smile crossed her lips, and she slept on.

"Mama's here," Victoria replied in a hushed tone. "Mama's here. All is well." She kissed Alana's cheek, turned from the room, and went back downstairs. Although the orange had long since left the living room, Victoria knew it was still there, just waiting for twilight to work its magic tomorrow, exposing all the warmth it could give. She would wait for its return as she would wait for the return of her husband as

Forgive Us Our Sins

Every morning at the stroke of 3:00 a.m., God smote Clifford Parsons awake. "Get your lazy ass out of bed," God said in a clear voice. "And don't even think about giving me lip. You're the laziest man I ever made." God sat on the wicker chair in a corner of Clifford's bedroom and shined purple. As often as he saw it, the glow always scared Clifford into obedience. He wasted no time throwing off the covers.

Frigid Lake Superior air filled the room, and although it was the middle of August, Clifford's feet balked at the touch of the cold pine floor. He reached for yesterday's blue shirt and brown britches hanging on the bedpost and fished his dirty socks off the floor. His hand brushed the King James Bible laying face down. It must have slipped from his hands when he fell asleep last night. He grabbed it and headed downstairs. God wasn't happy until Clifford was kneeling by the pink ottoman in the living room. God's instructions were so clear Clifford dared not veer from them.

This room, too, was cold, but God insisted no fire be lit until the praying was done. Clifford got right to it. He knelt, buried his head in his hands, and asked forgiveness for all his sins. Then he asked forgiveness for the sins of his wife, his daughters, all his relatives, friends, neighbors, and enemies. Then he asked God to forgive all the sinners in Pickford, Chippewa County, Michigan, the United States, North America, and the entire world. Each morning the list got longer and longer as Clifford thought of more and more people and places that needed forgiveness. It took a long time, but usually by 4:30 he had exhausted his list of supplications. Then he turned to the Psalms.

"Which one today?" he asked as he switched on the lamp by his chair.

"No Psalms this morning," God answered. "You're in a rut. Try Revelation."

Clifford was astounded. Revelation was for scholars, not for a man who hadn't made it past the eighth grade. "Are you sure?" he asked.

"Did I stutter? I said what I said. Revelation." The purple hue had worn off, and God wasn't scary anymore. Clifford couldn't see anything, but he felt the presence of a powerful force. It was everywhere. It filled the room. All the chairs and the Chesterfield, the bookshelves lined with Marion's unread collection of great authors, the knick-knacks, the pictures of living and dead relatives. God surrounded everything.

Clifford turned to the last pages of the Bible. He usually steered clear of this book. It didn't make any sense at all to the common man. He stretched his legs until his feet rested on the ottoman, and with one foot he pulled the turquoise afghan over the other. At this point, God didn't mind if he got comfortable and tried to warm himself. Clifford had at least another hour in front of him. He reached for the magnifying glass in the drawer of the table to his right.

"The Revelation of Jesus Christ, which God gave unto him, to show unto his servants things which must shortly come to pass; and he sent and signified it by his angel unto his servant John: Who bare record of the word of God, and of the testimony of Jesus Christ, and of all things that he saw. Blessed is he that readeth, and they that heareth the words of this prophecy, and keep those things which are written therein: for the time is at hand." Clifford perked up. These first lines didn't say anything about understanding what he was reading. They just said he'd be blessed for reading them. He could handle that. Maybe this wouldn't be so bad after all. If he admitted the truth, he was getting a little bored with the Psalms. He'd been reading them for years. His favorite ones he could quote line for line. Others he didn't like at all.

"...and from Jesus Christ, who is the faithful witness, and the first begotten of the dead... What does 'first begotten of the dead' mean?" Clifford asked God.

"It means what it says."

"But how can something be 'begotten of the dead'? That doesn't make sense. The dead don't beget anything."

"Look, Pal. You can't question every line. Just read the damn stuff. I don't know what half of it means either. I was high when I sent the revelation to my buddy, John, and he was none to sober either. Remember? He'd just escaped from a pot of boiling lard. You can imagine the state he was in."

"But that's not right. If you don't understand it, how will anyone else?"

"You're beginning to try my nerves. Imagine this—someone dies. You bury the corpse. Do you really think that's the end of it? Do you? If you do, then there's no point wasting my time on you. I'll speak real slow: What you bury is the corpse. Get it? A corpse can't beget anything, you're right, but what gave life to that corpse in the first place?"

"Oh, you mean what Jesus said, 'The flesh counts for nothing; it's the spirit that gives life.' That's what you mean, right?"

"Bingo. Now, just get on with it. I don't have all day." Clifford rearranged himself in the deep cushioned chair. He read on and on, mispronouncing words, skipping others, comprehending bits and pieces, ignoring cryptic verses. The pictures on the pages helped him imagine the images depicted by the words. It was close to six before he knew it, and God was gone. In his place stood Marion, wrapped in a plaid flannel nightshirt. The look on her face said it all. Her arms were crossed on her chest, and a twitch was working its way up her neck. He closed the book.

"You old fool," she said. "You haven't even started the fire. It's freezing in here." She grabbed the Bible from Clifford's hands and ripped out a few pages. She threw these into the kitchen woodstove along with a handful of cedar kindling. She lit a match and watched things jump to life, but the flame wasn't strong. She added more pages and blew on the fire. Once the kindling caught, it didn't take long for more flames to shoot up. She added dry sticks until the fire was going good. Then she placed a stick of birch on top. The papery skin burned quickly, and the fire was well on its way. A small piece of oak went in next. She closed the damper a bit, left the stove, and walked to the sink. She ran cold water into the granite coffee pot, measured in some grounds and a dash of salt, and set the pot on the stove.

"Watch this while I get dressed. Do you hear me, you old fool? Don't let that coffee boil over." Marion shook her finger at Clifford as if he were a toddler, instead of a man of 53. She flung the Bible at him. "Put that damn thing away and get to work. You think the cows will open the gate, walk in the barn, and milk themselves? You think the pigs don't need feeding? The chicken's going to lay without scratch? Get off your rear and get going. Whatever I saw in you is a mystery to me. You're an old man, homely as a stump fence, full of arthritis, but you're the cross I must bear. God, give me strength." The barrage continued as she mounted the stairs. Each word fell like a blow on Clifford's head.

As Marion thumped away, he knelt by the table and asked God to forgive her. He prayed for the salvation of her soul. He was ashamed of her. It wasn't the first time she had desecrated God's holy book. She was a hypocrite and a sinner. He wasn't judging her. He was speaking the truth, hard as that was. Usually he had finished reading and was at the barn by the time she awoke. It always angered her to catch him reading the Bible or praying. He figured it made her feel guilty, but nobody was stopping her from doing the same thing and getting herself saved. Clifford prayed every day that she would come to know Jesus and leave the Catholic Church, which in his eyes was nothing but a cult with the pope as Grand Dragon.

He checked the coffee. It wasn't ready yet, but the stove was hot enough to toast bread. He cut two thick slices from the white loaf on the counter. Before placing them on the stovetop, he wiped it clean with a piece of newspaper, then threw the paper in the stove and put the bread on top. It didn't take long for the slices to brown. He flipped each one and when both sides were golden brown, he spread them with butter and blueberry jam. The coffee was ready and smelled good. Just before it came to a boil, he lifted the pot and poured himself a cup. He sat at his place and bowed his head.

"Thank you, Jesus, for this good food. Bless the hands that picked these berries. Bless the farmer who grew the grain for this bread, and bless the miller who ground it. Bless the cow that gave the milk for the butter, and bless the dairyman who changed the milk into butter. Bless the factory worker who made this knife with which to spread the butter and jam upon this bread. Bless the man who made the chair upon which I sit and the table at which I eat. Bless yourself for giving me teeth to chew this good food and tastebuds to taste it. Bless you, too, for giving me a throat to swallow this meal and a stomach to churn it up and make it useful to all the parts of my body that need it. Bless the little Puerto Rican who grew these coffee beans and the grocer who sold them to me. Bless the sugar canes that provided this sweet sugar and bless the poor souls that harvested the canes. Bless everyone and everything on your good earth, and grant peace to this house. Amen." He spooned sugar into the coffee, stirred until the grains dissolved. Then he raised the cup and let the hot liquid trickle down his throat, warming his innards. He finished his toast and made two more pieces. He was buttering them when Marion came up behind him and hugged him. Clifford spun around as if he'd been touched by hot coals.

"Is that for me, Sugar Pie?" she asked. She had washed her face and put on her Jezebel rouge. The odor of cheap cologne covered her. Her red hair was pulled into a ponytail like a teenager's. Her fingernails were painted bright red. Her pleated housedress was unbuttoned too far, exposing her cleavage. When she walked, her hips swung like an open barn door. She became more a harlot with every step. She ignored Clifford's startled reaction, filled her cup, took the chair across from him, and smiled. "Do you want some sugar? Do you, you naughty boy?" She taunted him as she stroked her bountiful cleavage. "These ladies are waiting for you," she said. She leaned forward, her elbows pressing into the green oilcloth, her horn-rimmed glasses reflecting Clifford's disgust.

"I'm going to the barn," he said. He didn't trust himself to remain in her presence. He might strike her.

"You bastard," she called after him. "You're no more a man than the dead flies on the windowsill."

"Face it, Ma," their daughter, Louise, said. "He's not interested in you anymore now that he's found Jesus. Why not divorce him? You sure don't love each other." She plunked herself in Clifford's chair, finished his toast, and drank his coffee. Her pale eyes were outlined with dark blue pencil. Her cheeks were already rouged and her lips were painted a frosty coral. Maybe she had slept that way, or maybe she had just gotten home from spending the night with a boyfriend. She ran one hand through her tangled auburn hair, trying to straighten the snarled curls. "Admit it. You'd be better off without him. He doesn't even fight with you anymore. He just shuts up and prays and that's worse than yelling." She slapped her bedroom slipper on the back of her heel as she crossed one knee over the other and waited for a response.

"What do you know about it? You don't know anything." Marion's voice was strong, but calm.

"I know more than you think."

"What do you mean?" Marion stopped running hot water in the sink, turned and looked at Louise. She couldn't possibly know about Teddy. They'd always been careful to avoid each other's eyes at church gatherings, although their hands might casually brush against one another.

"Just what I said. I have eyes. You two hate each other."

Marion was visibly relieved. Her secret was safe. No one must ever discover her affair with the priest. Both of them would be run out of town. Then where would she be? An affair was one thing, but it couldn't compare to the security her husband gave her even if she did have to put up with his crazy religious ways.

"It's not hate," she said in a voice that sounded sincere. "It's not that at all."

"Then what is it?"

"It's living. Just plain old living." Marion finished washing the few dishes and placed them on the drainboard. She hung the dishrag on the faucet. She straightened a bow on the kitchen curtain. Just act normal, she told herself. Just act normal.

"What you do isn't living, Ma. It's barely surviving."

"How old are you, Louise?"

"Eighteen. You know that."

"Eighteen? And what have you got to show for yourself except a big mouth?"

"What's wrong with you, Ma? You're acting strange."

"It doesn't concern you."

"I heard you two fighting."

"We weren't fighting."

"Well, what would you call it?"

"I told you—living." Marion took another piece of maple from the woodbox. She opened the stove and threw it in.

"You're crazy, positively certifiable. We should send you to the hospital in Newberry. Maybe we should send Dad with you."

"You're an awful girl, Louise. Worse than your sisters. At least they had the good sense to leave home after they disgraced us."

"You sound old, Ma. I never heard you sound that way before."

"I'm 50 and feel 100," Marion said. She was on safe ground now. She breathed a sigh of relief, which Louise took as defeat. She might as well continue. "I'm old and worn out. Nobody cares a toss about me one way or the other. The only one who really loved me was Todd."

"You miss him, don't you?"

"Don't you?"

"Yeah, but not like you do. He was good to me, but he was better to you. Too bad he was killed in that car accident. He'd have made a nice son-in-law for you to make up for the awful daughters you raised."

"I'm going for a drive."

"Want me to go with you?"

"No."

"Where you going?"

"I don't know. Into town, maybe. Might stop by Todd's grave."

"When will you be back?"

"When I get here." Marion grabbed her purse and rifled through it. Good. There were a few dollars in it and some change. She had enough to buy gas. She turned to go.

"Ma, you know I love you, don't you? I know you're not crazy."

"And you're not awful all the time."

"Truce?"

"Truce."

After she left, Louise refilled her cup. Ma doesn't fool me, she thought. She only thinks she does. Louise flipped through a copy of "Screen Play," finished her coffee, left the cup on the chrome table, and fed her green parakeet, Rowdy. She opened his cage, and he flew from picture to picture, getting his morning exercise. Todd had given her two birds, but Rowdy had killed his green brother within a couple days. Now he was king. He flew to her shoulder as she held a piece of toast for him to peck. He dropped more crumbs than he ate. She brushed them from her chest. "That's enough," she said. "I'm going back to bed. Be a good boy." She petted his head and put him back in his cage.

"Blessed is he whose transgression is forgiven, whose sin is covered. Blessed is the man unto whom the Lord imputeth no iniquity, and in whose spirit there is no guile." Clifford quoted the Bible in a monotonous drone as he finished the milking. "Look not on our sinfulness, oh Lord, but on our weaknesses and grant us your strength to survive each day. Forgive us our sins. Sanctify us. Deliver us from the hands of the devil. Bless us and keep us safe. Guide our paths." His voice droned on and on, filling the brisk morning air with his pleas. Occasionally, one of the pigs grunted in response, but the cows remained silent witnesses to his preaching. They'd heard it all before.

Marion drove north on M-129, turned left on Six Mile Road, and headed for Teddy's place. She'd have to get there before he said daily mass. She turned the radio louder and pressed a little harder on the gas pedal. She sang with the music as her eyes filled with tears. "Happy days are here again, the sky above is clear again..."

Why does sin come so naturally to me, she wondered as she sped towards the church. Why? But like so many other questions, this one, too, had no answer.

Crowded Aisles at Callaghan's Market

The old, young-looking man pushed his grocery cart down the crowded aisles of Callaghan's Market in Sault Ste. Marie. It was the third of the month, the date when many retirees receive their Social Security check. I assumed he was retired but had yet to acquire a stooped back, rotund belly, or chicken-like neck found on so many male retirees. He actually looked quite dapper. His gray blazer was over a white shirt. His blue tie was in a spectacular Windsor knot. His black trousers were wrinkle-free and deeply creased. His white hair was immaculately cut, his gray beard perfectly trimmed, and his rimless spectacles of the latest style. I'm a young man and hoped I would look as debonair as he when I reached retirement age.

I had seen him a number of times as I did my shopping, but we had not exchanged pleasantries. I turned down the soup aisle where he was consulting his list. I watched as he checked it against whatever he wanted, comparing prices, checking and rechecking the stock hoping, perhaps, to find a bargain, a little something extra to bring home and surprise his wife or cat or whomever he lived with. He was totally immune to me and had he not unwittingly rammed my cart, I probably would have thought no more of him than one remembers old people anywhere.

"Oh, I'm sorry," he apologized. "I'm afraid I didn't see you. Please excuse me." He leaned towards me, then away, then forward again, not knowing if I was offended by the ram or him or whether I was offended at all. I left him guessing and stared at his remarkable face. I offered no comment or gesture to suggest what was in my mind. How could I confess I was facing a man who could have passed for the twin of my recently deceased and much loved aunt? I was mesmerized and astounded by his blue eyes that seemed to penetrate to the very marrow of my bones. I could not speak and my silence confused him.

"Young man," he said. "Excuse me. I didn't see you." He held a can of Campbell's Vegetable Soup in one hand and a can of Tomato in the other. He stood in the middle of the aisle trying to decide which one to put in his cart. I continued to stare, spellbound by this man making what was undoubtedly the most important decision of his day. This scion of a man who once, perhaps, had made life and death decisions. Who once, maybe, was responsible for dozens of employees. Whose job, perhaps, might have been to make laws or change them. This gentleman was now lost, as it were, in the middle of an ordinary supermarket aisle, unable to decide which canned liquid to buy for his table. He replicated Aunt Nora. It wasn't the stranger standing before me I saw, but my aunt who had once been a pillar of strength and beauty. It was in memory of her I was shopping at Callaghan's, her favorite market. By now a group of retired folks had gathered around us.

"The man said he was sorry," one of the ladies said. "Are you deaf?" She poked her index finger into my chest. Although she was thin, she was strong. I recoiled from her touch.

"What's the matter with you?" asked another. "Are you too good to accept his apology?" This woman was round and plump as a watermelon. Her green coat and hat caused her to look like she belonged in someone's garden. Her ruddy coloring resembled the flesh of a melon. Her black eyes were the seeds.

"Young man, you should be ashamed of yourself," was the response from the lady behind me. This woman, dressed in purple, was an eggplant. These shoppers were joined by others and encircled me. Some had cauliflower hair. Others were as yellow as wax beans. I was surrounded by a field of pumpkins, parsnips, radishes, and onions. The smell of rotting produce engulfed me. Each person became a vegetable daring me to say something in acknowledgement of the rammer's apology. They wanted to hear some words that would right the wrong I had committed by not speaking and which would allow them to return to their task at hand, undoubtedly the highlight of their day. And as I thought about it, I knew I should say something, that being the most courteous, expeditious thing to do, but somehow I couldn't. I opened my mouth but nothing came out. Someone called for the manager. I saw a red-jacketed tomato pushing his way through the crowd. "What's going on here?" he demanded. "Who started this racket?" He stood in front of me, hands on his hips, a smirk on his lips.

"He did," said the rammer. "He was stealing from my cart. He should be thrown out of the store or arrested."

"That's right," agreed the garden of the aged. "We saw him do it." They moved closer to the rammer, uniting against me. Due to chronology, I was the young outsider shopping during their time. These perfectly normal folks turned on me as if I had committed an unpardonable crime.

"Throw him out," a carrot yelled.

"Take his groceries," cried a zucchini.

"Send him to the end of the checkout line all day," suggested a celery stalk.

"Shoot him," shrieked a russet potato.

My heart beat faster as the garden closed ranks. I finally found my voice. "What's all the fuss?" I asked. "It was just a simple misunderstanding. Neither this gentleman nor I saw each other and our carts rammed. No stealing. No ramming on purpose. Nothing to bother about. Nothing at all."

"Liar!" screamed the rammer. His face was close to mine. I saw red veins shooting across his eyes. He was no longer Aunt Nora. He was a gray Hubbard squash.

"Liar!" said a grandmotherly type standing next to me with a plastic bag dangling from her arm. She became a replica of my aunt who died a week ago and whose funeral I had just attended.

"Liar!" bellowed a yam. "Dirty, rotten liar."

"But I'm not lying," I tried to explain.

"Leave the store immediately," the red tomato bellowed. "Leave the store before I call security."

"He can't leave until he apologizes," the Hubbard squash said. "I demand an apology."

Dozens of eyes turned on me, each with their own story of youth that had passed without stopping or stopped just long enough to tempt them, then moved on. The gray brows were knit together or missing altogether leaving only a ridge where age had eaten them away. Some cheeks were sucked in and withered, a crisscross mosaic that Klee or Picasso could have woven into a breathless design, but without the aid of an artist, the faces remained trapped in an unstoppable stage of decay. A few had yet to reach the age or attitude that indiscriminately forces lines through the forehead and around the mouth, digging into the once taut flesh. Their round, pink or pallid faces were naked, stripped of youth's freshness yet not quite ready to admit defeat. There were stained teeth, sinuous necks, sunken eyes, white hair, no hair, old breath.

My knees buckled and I held on to my cart. "Air," I said, "Give me air," but the knot of humanity held together, united in old age as, perhaps, they had failed to unite in youth. "I need air," I tried again, griping the cart tighter, feeling moisture form underneath my armpits and behind my knees. No one moved or spoke. The electric clock above the meat counter buzzed louder and louder. The checkout clerks beat furiously at their cash registers. The stock boys pounded cans together as if they were cymbals. The non-forgiving sea of eyes pierced me, encircled me, dared me to move. My desire for air, for the fresh, clean pure air of an early morning stroll in the countryside or along the St. Marys River where things live and die without notice or indignation was overwhelming, but the crowd refused to yield.

I slumped to the floor, landing amid orthopedic shoes and varicose veins. A cane poked me. A wheelchair crushed my hand. Time dragged, a minute, an hour, all the same. "Air," I repeated. "I need air." The ghastly odor of arthritic creams and rubbing alcohol gagged me. The pancake funeral powder and hairspray burned my eyes and my nostrils, bringing me first to the sick bed of my aunt, then to her coffin. I grabbed the small rubber wheels of my cart, my head dropping to my chest, fighting my mind's vision of Aunt Nora who was part of my flesh, too. In the faces around me, the vegetables disappeared. I saw only my aunt's smile, her neatly folded hands and the rosary she held as she awaited death in the hospital bed. She requested I bring her an Edgar Allan Poe book containing cryptic tales that was beside her nightstand at her home, but I had forgotten. It was the only thing she had ever asked of me, and the memory of her kind, expectant face anxiously waiting for the book each day I visited hung in my memory. I felt the warm touch of her hands, saw the gray, patient eyes and the loving smile. She never mentioned the book again. She died with the unfulfilled request suspended between us. The guilt strangled me. "I'm sorry." The words tumbled out at last. "I'm sorry, sorry, sorry."

Somewhere down another aisle or far away in another place and time, a child cried for his mother, the tiny voice surprisingly shrill and insistent, quieted only when the parent gave in to its demands for a cookie or a bag of chips. At the pastry counter a request came for apple turnovers. Someone at the meat counter wanted two T-bone steaks. I could breathe now. The garden had disbanded, their morning excitement over to be put aside and rehashed later that afternoon when they had tea with a spouse or a friend. I rose to my feet. I breathed deeply, anxious to walk into October's raw wind, to get away from the carnival of brightly colored ketchup bottles, rouged cheeks, bloody steaks, yellow teeth, slimy fish.

My heart stopped beating wildly. I regained a sense of decorum and saw the people walking away as individuals instead of vegetables. Ahead of me walked the rammer, his head proudly perched on his shoulders, his step light on the clean floor. I watched as he looked at his list and continued comparing prices, putting an item in the cart then withdrawing it and returning it to the shelf. He glanced back. His lips spread in a wide smile. Then I heard a voice cry out as the sound of clashing carts echoed down the aisle. I left my cart where it was and ran to the exit, willing myself not to look back. I inhaled the autumn air and realized I had been carrying guilt for no reason. It wasn't the book Aunt Nora had wanted. It was me, a request I had faithfully fulfilled. By visiting her every day, if only for a few minutes and bringing her an apple or an orange from Callaghan's Market, she knew she was loved beyond measure. If I had disappointed her in any way, I now knew all was forgiven.

Talk On, Jade Bea

God only give one gift to my wife, Jade Bea Greene, and that were the gift a' gab. She come outta the womb a hollerin' and a squawkin' and she been on auto-talk ever since. But the past few days, I's noticed a change in Jade Bea. Somethin' appears to be eatin' her. She ain't her normal self. She ain't said no more'n a handful a words, and when I ask what's wrong, she shakes her head and says she ain't quite sure. I thought it was some woman complaint, but she ain't never complained about such things afore and I doubt she'd start now. No, it's somethin' deeper'n that. She's hurtin' somewhere I can't quite reach to comfort her so this is what I did. I got in the pick-up and drove to Pickford early this mornin' to the dry goods store and bought her a new sun bonnet. It's made a straw and there's a tie around it so the wind won't blow it off when she's putterin' in her garden. And I got a new pair a garden gloves for her, too. I think she'll perk up when she sees her presents 'cause I don't recall buyin' her much a anythin' unless you count the hay baler I bought Mother's Day last month, and you can pretty much guess who that was for.

When I opened the kitchen door a few minutes ago, the place had a unhealthy quiet to it. The kitchen's spotless. Breakfast dishes washed and put away, dough's risin' for today's bread, and the red-and-white linoleum's shinin' like it's just had a fresh coat a wax. Everythin' looks normal, but that awful quiet's makin' me nervous. Usually, the radio's on and Jade Bea's singin' some old Hank Williams' song, but not this mornin'. It's death-like still. I take off my boots and put 'em on the bench, then I put my packages on the table, bein' careful not to mess up the new red tablecloth with the chickens dancin' around the border, and then I head down the hall.

"Jade Bea, Jade Bea," I call. "Where is you, Honey?" I looks in the front room, but it's empty and so's the far-front room. I check her sewin' room. Empty, too. The door to our bedroom's closed. That door ain't never closed and my chest gets a tight feelin'. I steady myself against the door, then turn the knob. There she is, lyin' flat on her back on our bed. She's wearin' a blue-and-white housedress with a blue apron over it. Her white hair's spread around the pillow, not in the bun like she always wears it. Her eyes are closed, and she looks for all the world like she's dead. Her hearin' ain't so good any more so I bend over and get real close to her left ear.

"Jade Bea! Is you still with me? Can you hear me, Baby?" I commence to shakin' her shoulders, real gentle. She opens one hazel eye and then the other. She looks at me like I ain't quite there. It takes her a minute to focus.

"Is that you, Hank?"

"'Course it is. Who else would it be? What's the matter with you, Baby?" She shakes her head as if to clear it.

"I had company after you left," she says. "I guess they wore me out." She leans back on the pillow. Her little shrunken face is white as cotton and looks even paler next to the bright pink pillowcase. Her teeth is restin' on the nightstand, and her little cheeks is sunk in her face. She's scarin' me.

"Who was here?" I sit on the side a the bed and reach for her hand. I never noticed how tiny it is, how skinny and full a blue veins. It's lost in my big rough one.

"It was them Jehovah Witnesses. I couldn't get rid of them."

"You didn't let 'em in, did you?" We never open our door to that bunch. "Did you, Jade Bea? Did you go against the rules?"

"Well, I wasn't intending to, but you know how they are. They caught me off guard. I'd finished waxing half the kitchen floor when there was a loud knock and without thinking I yelled 'come in' and in they come. I couldn't get rid of them." She acts like that little bit a talk wore her out and turns her head towards the window. The white pines is swayin' in the breeze, and a big crow's perched on the top branch of a dead tree, surveyin' the ground for his lunch. Jade Bea watches him until he flies away, then turns back to me. "They wouldn't let up, Hank. They kept badgering and badgering about Jehovah and His chosen ones. I asked them to leave, but they wouldn't." Her voice gets soft and trails off. It's like she run outta words—like the last few quiet days been leadin' up to this moment. I can feel part a Jade Bea driftin' away. I got to do somethin'.

"Mrs. Greene," I says. "You's a good woman. You ain't got to take to your bed on account a no Jehovah Witness. They ain't worth it. Now, stir yourself and fix my lunch." Usually when I calls her Mrs. Greene she knows I don't know what else to say, but I'm in her corner. It don't work this time, though. She just lays back on them soft pillows, looks at all them pines we planted 45 years ago, and don't say another word. "I'm gonna have to call the vet, if you don't rally soon, Mrs. Greene. What you say about that?" Still she don't say a word. "The vet, Mrs. Greene. I'm talkin' Doc Willard. You want me to call him? You want him pokin' and pryin'?" I reach for the phone on the bedside table and pretend I'm dialin' some numbers.

"Hank, you old fool. You don't know his number any more than I do. I'll get up in a minute." That's her way a dismissin' me. I put down the phone.

"Don't you wanna know where I been all mornin'?"

"I thought you were at the barn."

"I been shoppin' over to Pickford. Bought you some presents, but you can't see 'em until you get outta bed. I'll be waitin' in the kitchen. Them loaves you got risin' is nearly ready for the oven."

She pats my hand like I's two years old. "Just give me a minute. Just another minute and close the door on your way out." Then she's quiet again and I can't hardly stand it.

I go back to the kitchen. The red electric clock hangin' above the oak table says it's half-past noon. No wonder my belly's hollerin'. I ain't had nothin' since eggs and ham and coffee at six this mornin'. I ain't got much to get up for, but I can't sleep no later'n six. Been a early riser all my life. Jade Bea's the same. The four boys are growed and gone—none was interested in the farm. Too much work, too little profit, and they all liked their beds. A farmer ain't got no time to sleep in the mornin'. The boys don't write much, and we ain't seen 'em in a year, not since our grandson, Lyle, died and the boys come home for his funeral.

Lyle's mother were our only daughter. We called her Eve. She were a pretty little thing—looked just like Jade Bea—but she were a wild one, worse than the boys. She might a been okay if that Steele boy from one sideroad over had left her alone. He come home from the Army when Eve was 15, and he come sniffin' around our place. She took a likin' to him. He lit outta town when she told him she was carryin' his child. She were in labor 36 hours afore she birthed Lyle. When he finally come out, Eve was so tired she closed her eyes and never opened 'em again. We didn't tell Lyle who fathered him. Maybe that were wrong, but it's too late now. Early one Saturday mornin' nigh on to a year ago, Lyle took the canoe from the shed and put 'er in the river, somethin' he'd done a hundred times or more when he wanted to fish. Only this time he didn't come home. He were only 13 and the apple of our eyes.

Things ain't been the same around here without him. Nobody knows why he drowned. The river was high, it bein' spring, and overflowed its banks. The current was swift, but Lyle knew that river well enough to know when it was safe and when to draw back. There were some talk he did it on purpose, but I put a stop to that line a thinkin'. There's enough gossip in a small town like Brimley without the locals makin' sport of a young boy's unfortunate passin'. We was gonna build a rabbit hutch from the remains of the old chicken coop. That's what we'd planned to do that day as soon as he come back with a rope a suckers for our supper. Well, it don't do no good dredgin' up things. I shake myself and do somethin' useful. I check the loaves. Yep, they's ready for the oven. In the old days, the stove'd be roarin' and I'd throw the pans in and keep addin' more wood 'till the bread baked. But Jade Bea wanted a new *range*, as the salesman at Wards called it, so I moved the woodstove to the basement and set up this here *range* in its place. That were five years ago, and I ain't figured out how to run the dang thing yet.

"Jade Bea, Baby. These loaves gonna fall if'n you don't get up and bake 'em." I yell from outside the bedroom door, somethin' I ain't never done afore. "Do you hear me, Baby? All your work'll be for nothin'. You hear me, Jade Bea Greene?" She answers from behind the closed door.

"Yes, I hear you, Hank," she says, and opens the door so fast she musta been standin' right behind it. "For the first time in all our years together I hear you loud and clear." She don't even look at them loaves, just walks to the table and pours herself a cup a cold coffee and stirs some sugar in it, but she don't drink it. She sits in the chair across from me.

"That's what them Witness people taught me this morning. They taught me to hear. I believe that's why God sent them while I was on my knees scrubbing our floor. Imagine, the Witnesses finding me on my knees." She shakes her head as if to shake away the picture that's stuck in it. 'Though your sins be red as scarlet, I shall make them white as snow.' That scripture came to me when I turned around and saw them two standing inside my house. 'Though your sins be red as scarlet...'" Her voice trails off and I can't stand it. Jade Bea ain't one to feel sorry for herself. This ain't the woman I married—my Jade Bea don't snivel.

"Catch a holt a yourself, Mrs. Greene," I tell her. "You ain't got no sins, so shake off this mood. You got to put aside this kind a thinkin' and get these loaves in the oven. And open your presents and see what I brung you."

"Let me be, Hank. I've got to think this through. When I finally told them Witnesses to get out of my house or I'd call the law, they left. Then I took the tracts one of them placed on the counter, went to the basement, threw them in the woodstove, and watched them burn. I finished scrubbing the floor, but that line from the Bible kept running through my head, and I couldn't ignore it. Over and over it played in my mind until I took to our bed."

"Mrs. Greene," I starts to say, but she silences me with a wave a her hand.

"I got to change, Hank, but I don't know how. I been one way for so long, no other way comes natural. Lately, something in my spirit's been nagging me. It's no wonder the boys left. Who'd want to stick around a place where there's no peace and quiet unless you're alone in the outhouse? I see my life for what it's been—talk, talk, talk—plenty of talk but nothing to say. And when did I ever listen? I see now where I made my mistake. I should of kept my mouth shut and my ears open. Maybe the boys would still be here and maybe Eve and Lyle would still be alive." Her face crumples up and tears come runnin' down her cheeks like a stream headin' for a lake. I don't say nothin'.

"I miss them all. Sometimes I hear Lyle's voice carrying on the wind when I'm in the garden and I look up expecting to see his sweet face, but he's not there, and he won't ever come back." Jade Bea lays her face on her arms and cries hard. In all our years together, I ain't never seen the like. "Hank," she says when she calms down. "Have you been happy with me? Have you?"

I take her hand in mine. "Baby, you know I have. Now stop this nonsense and bake the bread. God's the one who made you the way you are and He ain't gonna punish you for usin' somethin' He give you. He give you the gift a gab. Don't you be returnin' it." I squeeze her hand and she squeezes back. "Your talk don't hurt nobody. It's just talk for the sake a hearin' a clear voice fill the air. I'd be lost without it and so would the robins and wrens and chickens and trees and everythin' else you gab to." She gets up and turns on the oven.

"I never thought of talk as a gift. Do you think you could be right?"

"Have you ever knowed me to be wrong?"

"No," she says. She uncovers the loaves and sprinkles water and salt on the tops a each afore she puts 'em in the oven. "Turn on the radio," she says, then she sits at her place and opens the bags. She tries on the hat and admires herself in the little mirror hangin' on the wall.

"It's perfect," she says and slips her hands into the gloves. "Perfect, too."

"You okay?" I ask, and she nods.

"I'll fry some potatoes," she says and with her hat still on, she commences peelin' the spuds. Pretty soon, the kitchen starts to smell like a bakery from the smell a hot bread. I take a piece a cedar from my shirt pocket and whittle. A breeze brings the caw of a crow through the open window.

"That's a pretty sound," says Jade Bea. "It reminds me of a one-eyed crow I saved from certain death when I was a child. It was just about this time of year, and I was helping Pa dig post holes for the new fence he was going to put around Ma's vegetable garden. When I moved my boot to step over what I thought was a cow pie, I saw a tiny black speck of something on the ground. I reached over and picked it up and there he was—that one-eyed Jack—and Pa told me I'd better be careful not to squish him, and he also said be careful not to get pecked, but I wouldn't listen and..."

I close my eyes and hear the sound a Jade Bea's beautiful voice fillin' the space around us, and I know today's gonna be another good day.

December's Quarry

The Sachels moved into an abandoned Airstream in Gulliver near Manistique when Tommy was seven years old, one day before the Japanese bombed Pearl Harbor. Pa had driven to Michigan from Kentucky and for the first time in his life Tommy was going to live in a house on land. No more Ohio River for him. No more houseboat. Just land and grass and trees and solid ground wherever he stepped. Nothing would remind him of the life his family was leaving behind except the empty spot at the table where his youngest sister should have been. Penny died in a fire a railroad man caused when he threw some live clinks into what he thought was the river, but turned out to be the Sachel's houseboat. Pa managed to save all the kids except Penny. Every day he blamed himself for her death, and nothing Ma or anybody else said could comfort him. Now it looked like they would have a new home, and Tommy thought everything was going to be great.

The Sachels had kin living in Detroit and after the tragedy Ma wrote and asked if they could come north. The relatives said yes, but they couldn't stay long because their house was already overcrowded with poor southern relatives who thought they'd make it rich in the big city, but never had quite enough money to find a place of their own. Pa said thank you, but he wouldn't look for work in a car factory. He was interested in logging and said they'd move farther north and not bother stopping in Detroit. Chum, the oldest child, was going to stay in Louisville where he had a job cleaning stables.

The rest of the family piled into a beat-up Chevrolet given to them by a preacher from the Shepherdsville Baptist Church. Pa drove US-41 from Kentucky to Michigan, boarded the ferry that crossed the Straits of Mackinac, arrived in the Upper Peninsula, got on US-2 and didn't stop until he reached a dirt road in Gulliver. By then they were out of gas and out of money so where the car stopped is where they stayed. The road was quiet and no houses were in sight. Pa got out and followed a trail leading to a clearing where he saw the abandoned trailer. He pushed the door open and looked around. The place was empty. He walked back to the main road and shifted the car into neutral. Ma steered while the others cheered and pushed it through the ruts.

"We're like the Snopes family," Ma said referring to characters in a Faulkner novel. "But we're a whole lot better." As the afternoon sun broke through the trees, Tommy thought she looked like an angel with her yellow hair around her shoulders and a few lazy snowflakes touching her face. He thought she was beautiful. Tommy didn't see the shabby cloth coat or the thin faded housedress it covered. He didn't know there were holes in her shoes, tears behind her smile, or that her belly yelled so his wouldn't. All he saw was his mother—a kind, gentle woman who held him when he had nightmares.

The Airstream was tiny, but someone had built a shed on the back of it and installed a small stove. Pa wasted no time filling it with twigs and large, dead branches. Soon the chill was off the place and rabbit stew bubbled in a cast iron pot. Pa had killed the rabbit with his rifle although it meant someone might hear the shot and come investigating. Tommy was proud of Pa and one day hoped to shoot as straight as his father. Tommy knew bullets cost money and money was hard to come by and a man had to make his kill on the first try. Ma took the sourdough starter and began making biscuits.

The dark fell fast. It covered everything so quickly the Sachels had to fumble in crumpled Piggly Wiggly bags to find candles. Pa lit them with Diamond matches he kept in the compass with the screw top. The compass was always in his shirt pocket. He was a tall man, tall and thin, with a wild bush of ink-black hair and eyes as blue as the sky. He had fine, straight teeth, a strong nose, and whiskers black as General Lee's boots. His hands could wring the neck of a turkey as easily as Tommy could squish an ant. They could pull sycamore roots out of the river when the oxen had given up. Tommy could feel their strength when Pa raised him to his shoulders, but he never felt their power on his behind, for like Ma, Pa was of a gentle nature. As the Sachels sat around the table, he asked a blessing on their food. He thanked his Maker for their shelter and promised to seek the owner in the morning. He would barter work for this living place. The Sachels were not freeloaders. They earned their keep. He prayed for a mild winter. When he stopped, quiet fell around the table as the family ate their first real meal in days. They ate slowly, relishing each bite.

When it was time for sleep, Tommy was sandwiched between his sisters on a worn out mattress. Ma and Pa chose the floor in the shed where they could feed the fire during the night. Just past midnight, Tommy awoke crying from another nightmare about Penny. He didn't think he had cried aloud, but Ma was there in a heartbeat. She picked him up and carried him to the shed. There was a chair near the stove. She held him and promised him everything would work out. Eventually Pa traded places with her. The rest of the night passed without further cries inside or out, and a new dawn brought a feeling of peace and hopefulness to the family.

Pa arose early, raked the embers to life, and added more dry branches mixed with some frozen birch logs he found stacked outside the shed. He heard a shot ring through the woods. He couldn't tell which direction it came from or how close it was to the trailer, but it wasn't long before he saw a deer running across the clearing. He raised his rifle and brought the animal down. As Pa and Tommy ran to the kill, they saw a man coming from the opposite direction. Van Rhoades owned the Airstream, the land it was on, and the deer Pa had just shot.

"Hello, there," Pa yelled. "I guess this is yours."

Rhoades walked out of the tangled bush. He tried to hide his embarrassment. Not felling a deer on the first shot was the sign of a poor hunter.

"You got that right," he said. "It must have picked up my scent. The thing sprinted as I fired." He knelt and looked over the buck. "Eight pointer," he said. "Lots of venison for the winter." His bullet had caught the deer's hind flank. Not enough to bring it down immediately, but more than enough to make it suffer. He paused for a minute, loosened his jacket, took a swig from his flask and offered it to Pa.

"Much obliged but no thanks," Pa said. "My name's Sachel. I suppose this is your land." The chest of Van Rhoades puffed with pride as he declared the land had been in his family for over 100 years, all 175 acres of it, and then he asked Pa how long he planned on staying in his Airstream.

Tommy's heart sank even before Pa said anything because he sensed they wouldn't stay long. It was the way Rhoades grunted as he leaned on his rifle which was leaning on the deer that was shot when deer hunting season had passed. The look on his face and the careless way he treated the animal told the child the man standing before him was unkind. Pa said he would work all winter, felling trees, toting water, mucking barns. Anything Van Rhoades needed doing, Pa would do if they could just winter in the Airstream. Tommy kept his eyes on the ground and tried not to listen. He tried even harder not to cry when he heard Pa pleading to stay.

Many years passed and Tommy grew old, but he never forgot the sound of Pa's voice on that bright December morning when he was told to move on. The voice Tommy loved was filled with the same tone he had heard the day Penny died. Two more times he was to hear what he came to know as the sound of anguish. A year later when a government man stopped by the shack they lived in near Manistique and gave Ma condolences because Chum had been killed in action, and the day Ma died. Some sounds are like that. They're unforgettable because they tug at your heart and echo through your mind.

The story of the Sachels is an old one. It's a story of poverty and struggle, two of life's greatest challenges, but it's also a story of love and fortitude. Some folks are defeated by hard times and circumstances. Others wade through them, convinced a better life is waiting just around the corner if only they have the strength to turn it. Were the Sachels able to do that? We'll never know.

Gone Too Long

Dickie Hicks had been gone too long from Granite Street in Marquette to call it home anymore although he still lived there. He shared the ranch style house with his wife of 14 years and their 14 year old son, Jimmy. The boy was why Dickie stayed. He felt it was his duty to remain in the family unit. He didn't actually take part in Jimmy's life. He never attended church services, and he went to the school's Christmas program only because Sheryl dragged him.

After years of drinking and cheating on his other wives, he'd found Sheryl and she'd given him a son to settle him down. Dickie was determined to stick this marriage out. He felt he owed her that much, but no more, even though she was the one who paid the bills. If truth be told, he didn't think he really owed Sheryl anything because Dickie was a selfish nitwit and pretense was his game. Now they sat facing each other as Jimmy lie motionless between them at Marquette General Hospital, his blue eyes closed forever. Dickie didn't know what to do, so as usual, he did nothing, leaving Sheryl to take the lead.

It had all happened so quickly. One minute Jimmy was alive and the next he was gone. An automobile accident. Nobody's fault. Just one of those bizarre things. Jimmy was riding with his cousin, Pughy, who was driving a little too fast on CR-492. It was a beautiful August day. A Sunday. The boys were listening to an Elvis CD. They were crazy about him. He had been dead for ten years by the time they were born, but Elvis touched them in a way no current singer could. They played his CDs endlessly. His music helped Jimmy forget about the tension at home. It was obvious his parents despised each other. Jimmy knew they stayed together because of him. He knew he couldn't fix their marriage and make them happy, but they didn't know it. They thought by staying together he wouldn't realize their marriage was a sham. Parents were stupid. "American Trilogy" was blasting when he opened the door and rolled out. That was all there was to it. Just a handsome young boy opening a car door and rolling to his death. The car behind them rolled over him.

Jimmy's beautiful face and strong body were broken. His wavy yellow hair looked so natural, so innocent as he lie on the road and his hair turned red. It was hard to believe he was gone. Even crushed, he looked like he might awaken at any minute. After he was taken to the hospital, it was only when the attending physician came into the room and placed his hand on Dickie's shoulders and said it was time for him to go home that he realized, unlike his son who was now in heaven, Dickie had no home to go to.

He leaned over Jimmy and kissed him. Then he looked at Sheryl, but he had to look away. Her blue eyes had turned to steel. She could no longer hide the hatred she had kept at bay so Jimmy wouldn't notice, but now that he was gone, there was no reason to hide her contempt. She could flaunt it or nourish it until it grew bigger than the room or the building or the town or the universe. She could feed and water her hatred as faithfully as she fed and watered her plants.

Fourteen years are a long time to hate someone and pretend you love him for the sake of your child. Fourteen years of a marriage that was one in name only. Dickie looked longingly at her, his brown eyes full of tears. Sheryl felt a pang of guilt. It was obvious Dickie was suffering as much as she was. Maybe she could put aside her contempt for him at least until Jimmy was safely in the ground. When she asked Dickie if he was going back to the house to get his things and move in with his girlfriend, he shook his head and suggested they go for coffee or a coke or even a drink. He knew she liked a glass of wine as much as he liked his whiskey.

Sheryl hesitated, then nodded. Dickie tried to take her hand, but she pulled it from him. Why bother now, she thought. Why pretend you want to hold any part of me now that I'm as broken as Jimmy? Why continue putting on a show for anyone who might be looking? Dickie followed her to her car. His truck was in the shop. It was always being repaired. He didn't have the $2,000 he owed the mechanic and until he could shake it out of Sheryl, the truck stayed where it was.

Once in a booth at Flannigan's, Dickie broke down. They hadn't spoken a word on the drive, each quietly blaming the other for Jimmy's suicide. It was too painful to admit their son had chosen to end his life. That at 14 he was done with living. Dickie wondered what had gone wrong, being too stupid to realize he was the primary reason. Sheryl ordered a glass of white wine. He ordered a whiskey and told the waiter to keep it coming. He planned to get plastered. There was no reason to try and remain sober now that there was no longer any need to set an example for the son who was no more. Sheryl gave him a look that sent shivers down his spine.

"No point in staying sober," he said.

"Was there ever?" she asked.

"I did it for the kid. For you and the kid. I never wanted him to see me drunk. You know that. And I didn't want to lose either of you."

"You did it for yourself. You've never done anything for anybody in your life." The hate that had roiled in Sheryl's heart for years spilled over and came raging through her mouth. "As far as losing us goes, you lost me the day Jimmy was born when you dropped me off at the hospital and went to the bar. You left us for three days. Three days I waited for you to sober up and come to the hospital. The day I gave birth to your son was the day I started hating you. Do you think I could start loving you on the day of his death?"

Dickie's head hung to his chest. Tears filled his eyes.

"Go ahead and cry. Cry like you always did when you watched strangers on television. You piece of filth. How many times did I watch you cry over a movie? Thirty times? Fifty? A hundred? Cry over a piece of fiction while I sat next to you and yearned to be held, to be told I was loved." Dickie reached for her hand.

"Don't touch me, you monster. It's because of you Jimmy is dead. It's because of you I'll never see my boy again. You drove him to his grave. You, with your bullshit talk to waitresses, sales clerks, receptionists, nurses, and any other woman you were near. Don't you think he felt my pain and anger when you spent more time flattering strangers than your own wife? Do you think he was as stupid as you? He knew every time you came home in a rage. He knew when you threw me across the living room. He knew I was terrified of you until I realized you're just a bully. A loser. A user."

"Please, Sheryl. Please stop."

"Do you have any idea how much I hate you?"

"Why?"

"Are you really so stupid you don't know?"

"You're the one with all the answers, Sheryl. You're the one with the education. You tell me."

"And you're the one with the Ph.D. in manipulation. In control. In pulling my strings and making me dance every time you said dance. Our life together has been nothing but a game to you, a way to pass the time. Something to keep you amused while you waited for someone better to come along. Is your new girlfriend richer, thinner, more agreeable than I am? Is she waiting for you now? How long do you think she'll put up with you when she finds out you don't have a nickel to your name and the only things you own are the clothes on your back and it was my money that paid for them?" Sheryl was on a roll now. She sat up straighter, felt stronger. She watched the blood drain from Dickie's face. For the first time since the night they met, she was in control. It felt good.

"I never wanted her or any of the others. It's always been you."

"Do you have any idea how many times I wanted to run a knife through your spine when you came home smelling of another woman?" Sheryl leaned back in the booth. Her grief had momentarily fled replaced by seething rage. She was a beautiful woman, always poised, always aware of her intelligence, but always fearful of Dickie's mood swings. Seeing him wilt before her, she was no longer afraid of the psychological mess he had always been. She felt no pity and would give no mercy. She laughed.

"I wish you had run a knife through me. I wish I'd never lived to see this day." Dickie slumped forward.

"And I wish you a long life. A long life filled with pain every time you breathe. I hope you see Jimmy's face every morning when you get up and every night before you go to bed. I hope he haunts you until the day you die." Sheryl left the booth. "You can walk back to the house," she said as she headed for the door. "Pick up your shit and get out of my life."

"Don't leave me," Dickie cried. "I love you."

"Need another drink?" the waiter asked. "Having a little trouble with your lady?"

"I need a bottle," Dickie said. "And send that pretty brunette over here. She's been eyeing me up since I walked in. Time she joined me."

"That's my wife," the waiter said. "The day I send her to you is the day you die."

"I'm ready," Dickie said, but he wasn't ready, not really. And he didn't want another drink or another woman. He wanted Sheryl. He left the bar, determined to talk sense into her. After all, she was his wife. She had to forgive him for all the affairs and mistakes he had made during their marriage. If she refused, he would make her. He knew he could win her over. His charm never failed him and if it did, there was always his fist.

When he stumbled crossing the parking lot, Sheryl was ready. She had no intention of killing him, just breaking his legs. As she knocked him down and ran over them, it was like going over a speed bump—barely noticeable at all. She called 911 and waited for the police to arrive. The performance she put on was worthy of an Academy Award. Now she was grateful they had played pretend for 14 years. No one would ever accuse the distraught woman of harming Dickie because no one knew the truth. She didn't follow the ambulance to the hospital. Instead she went home and packed his suitcase. Everything he had brought to the marriage fit in one case. It would be waiting for him when he was well enough to walk again.

She sensed Jimmy was proud of her and for the first time since his birth, she was proud of herself. She sat at the table and wept. The knowledge that the years ahead would be good ones were heartbreaking knowing that Jimmy would be a part of them only through her memories.

The Premature Passing of Howdy Blanks

It was 4:00 a.m. when Clayton Crats came pounding on my front door and hollering as if to wake the dead. "Howdy Blanks killed himself," he yelled. "He did it right this time. Get up, Link, and come take a look."

Now, any farmer in Goetzville will tell you, you don't go yapping and carrying on and waking a man from a sound sleep unless you're looking for trouble. Especially when it's a hot September night with nary a star to brighten the sky and the harvest moon is hidden behind the clouds. So when I heard Clay's scratchy voice breaking into my nice dreams about Diamond Lil, I sat bolt upright in the bed and thought my whole dang place was going up in flames. I reached for my britches and almost knocked myself out as I hit the rafter above me. If I had been a married man with a Mrs. and some little ones, we'd all have burned in our beds before I collected my wits.

Anyway, Clayton Crats is what you might call the town gossip. Every little town has one, even a one-horse burg like Goetzville. Usually it's a woman, some poor old widow who has nothing better to do than flap her jaws about everyone and everything in town. We had Clay. So when I heard him pounding on my door, I figured even he wasn't crazy enough to yell in the dark when whatever gossip he had to tell could wait until dawn which would soon be here. So I jumped into my britches and beat it down the stairs. Clay had let himself in and was half-way up with his dog, Jumper, nipping at his heels. "What in tarnation's going on?" I demanded. "Where's the fire?"

"There ain't no gall darn fire," Clay said. "It's Howdy Blanks. He's finally done what he's been threatening to do for 20 years ever since Beulah left him. I just came from his place and the crowd's getting too big for the shack to hold them."

Now I know to city folks a man trying to kill himself isn't big news, but in a little hollow like ours, it's front page news for two, maybe three weeks and maybe even longer depending on how he does it. I said a man *trying* to kill himself because Clay gets ahead of his story now and then, and I wasn't going to call Howdy dead until I saw him with my own two eyes. "Git, Jumper," I yelled at his mutt nipping at my ankle. "Now, Clayton, calm down and tell me what happened while the details are still fresh in your mind."

"Close as I can figure it, old Howdy got some sleeping pills and didn't stop until the whole darn bottle was empty. Me and Jake were out shinin' in Fred's Bush for that buck we saw yesterday when we heard Bulldog howling like his heart was broken. So I said to Jake we'd better check it out. It ain't like Bulldog to howl for nothing. By the time we got to Howdy's shack, he was lying stark naked in the middle of the kitchen floor. His eyes were big as plates and the empty bottle of pills was next to him and an empty bottle of Wild Turkey bourbon was next to it."

We're walking as he's talking and we're at his convertible. At least that's how folks around here refer to the contraption Clay made for himself. It's part tractor, part combine, part '53 Chevy and it rides like a hay wagon and looks like something you'd shoot if you saw it on a back road on a dark night. But it's the best Clay has and he's mighty proud of it. He jumped in the driver's seat and I cranked her up and off we went. Howdy's place is just south of mine on East Traynor. I reckon we could have walked in the length of time it took to get the old crate going, but I kept my yap shut and held tight as Clay chugged down the road with Jumper running alongside us.

As soon as Howdy's place came in view, I knew Clay was right. The lights were on and the shack was crawling with sightseers, old and young alike, and we had to fight our way through the crowd to get in. "Is he dead?" I asked, and no less than 23 people answered and not one said the same thing. "Is the man dead?" I tried again, and this time Jake broke through the mess of folks and came running over. I'll stop relating my story and tell you about Jake Toddle, Clay's kin. Jake's got one of them faces that looks like a roadmap. He isn't that old but there's plenty of miles showing on his mug. He's not the best looking feller in Chippewa County on a good day, but get a look at him in the early morning hours with his red mustache and baseball beard and those yeller-brown eyes rolling and those donkey ears sticking out from underneath his straw hat and I'm telling you, he'd scare a man who's been through war and seen the wrong end of a rifle pointing at him. So I don't have to tell you what passed through my mind when I laid eyes on Jake. It was written all over his face in the glare of the kitchen overhead light.

"Daid?" he says. "Daid? Of course he's daid. The man swallered a bottle of pills washed down with booze." Then he commenced to telling me that as soon as he heard Bulldog howling he knew what had happened. "I knowed it," he said. "Old Howdy didn't have a friend in the world and two days ago when I seed him, he were carryin' on like he were the only man in the county with problems. He like ta talk me ears off, he did, and went on and on tellin' me how his wife run off and took the little ones with her. I tried to tell him that were 20 years ago, but ta him it was yesterday. It didn't do no good tryin' to comfort him. I figure he finished off the bottle of Turkey tonight and when that didn't do the job, I figure he swallered the sleepin' pills. Dang shame, it is, to have a man kill himself for some fool woman who probably don't even remember his name. Dang, cryin' shame."

I left Jake rattling on and pushed my way to where they'd moved Howdy to his cot by the stove. I'm not one to criticize another man's home, but you've got to remember his shack wasn't any bigger than a good sized chicken coop and just about as dirty. There was a floor, alright, but covered with muck for so long nobody had seen it in years. We only knew it was there because we were standing on it. And the smell—it was something else. A body might be able to stand it if there was a strong wind blowing off Lake Superior, blowing in through the windows on a cool night, and blowing the smell right out the front door. Or if a person's nose only worked once in a while, it might not be too bad, but on a hot night with a house full of folks, there was no way in the world anybody was going to pretend Howdy's shack didn't stink. Years of birch wood mixed in with a whole lot of Prince Albert tobacco and smoked suckers and old feet and a wet dog and you'll get the picture. Your nose will head for the door long before your feet do.

Anyway, Howdy looked for all the world like he was just taking a nap and dreaming about wild turkeys. Someone went for the doc, but he hadn't come yet and being it was a no-account drunk like Howdy, he wasn't likely to come at all. I've been known to do a bit of doctoring myself. Course it's mostly a sick cow or a horse with colic, but I figured there can't be much difference between an animal and a human except maybe an animal's got a lot more sense. So I told the crowd to scatter and I knelt by Howdy's side. I don't have to tell you the smell of that old boy almost knocked me out, but I'm a tough old bird, too, and I knew if anybody was going to save him, it was going to be me.

"Howdy," I yelled in his ear. "Get up, you mangy old sot. Get up and get out of this gall darn bed." Of course, he didn't bat an eye as most dead folks don't, but I'm not one to give up without a fight. "Howdy," I tried again. "Howdy Blanks. Can you hear me? This here's Link Boggs, your friend and neighbor." But he just lay there with a little grin spreading on his lips and the whites of his eyes staring at me. He gave me the leaping jumps, but I ignored what I was looking at and pretended I didn't see him turning the prettiest shade of blue I ever saw.

That's when I remembered the time my best Holstein decided to chew on a bone one of my dogs had left in the field. I was fixing fence, and I saw that cow with her head reaching for the sky and her mouth hanging open with her tongue sticking out and a mess of foam dripping from it. I threw down the wire and hammer and lit out to save her. I knew she was choking even if at the time I didn't know on what. I grabbed the nearest branch from a sampling and stuck it down her throat. When it got down far enough, she commenced to coughing and that ratty old bone she'd been enjoying came right out with the rest of the grass and clover she'd had for breakfast. I sure breathed a sigh of relief when I saved her, and I figured I could do the same for Howdy.

As I looked at him, his color hadn't gotten any worse, and his chest was moving up and down like he still had some life left in him. "Get over here, Clay," I yelled, and Jake came with him. We turned Howdy on his side and thumped his back. Then we sit him up and a wee bit of pink began creeping over his scrawny neck. His pupils came back to the whites and he looked almost normal. Then I told Jake and Clay to hold him while I went outside and grabbed some rhubarb from the patch by the outhouse. I noticed the moon was trying to break through the clouds and fog was starting to cover the ground and the trees sparkled from a good night's rest. I heard one of Clay's cows moo and then another and then I hightailed it back to the shack where the crowd was getting drowsy, but still wouldn't go home.

I got a rusty pail that was leaning against the stove and emptied the ashes out of it. Then I snapped the leaves off the rhubarb. Then I told the boys to steady Howdy while I opened his yap and shoved the stalk as far down his throat and who knows where after that. As I said, I wasn't going to believe Howdy was dead until I saw him laid out at the undertakers. Once that rhubarb got wherever it was needed to go, it stopped. Then it unplugged Howdy. He lit up like a Christmas tree. His face still had a tinge of blue to it, but the pink had creeped all the way up to his chin. I got the pail ready and up come that rhubarb and some gawd awful stuff the likes of which I had never seen before and hope I never see again. Howdy carried on like that for five minutes and when he finished, he wiped his mouth with the back of his hand and bellered one word as strong as an ox, "Beuuuuulah." Then he laid his head on the little pine needle pillow. When he realized he was still alive he was madder than a wet hen. I said to him, "Howdy, I just saved your life and you're carrying on like you wish I'd let you go. Is that any way to show gratitude?" He looked at me, shook his head and said he was only a wee bit drunk and he didn't need help from anybody. Then he asked for Bulldog.

That's when I had to tell him the truth. "Howdy," I said. "Bulldog's gone. Seems in all the commotion we never gave him a second thought. When he saw Miss Violet's poodle, he fell in love. When she left, he left with her. I'm sorry to say, but I don't think you'll be seeing Bulldog again." That's when Howdy jumped off his cot, jumped into his britches, and chased me down the road. Chased me all the way to M-134. He swore he'd never forgive me for shoving that rhubarb down his throat or forgive Miss Violet's poodle. And believe it or not, that's how this story ends.

About the Author

Sharon's hallmark is her ability to portray fictional characters as if they were our friends and neighbors. This collection of short stories is an amusing and often poignant observation of people who populate small towns whether in Michigan's Upper Peninsula or elsewhere. Sharon writes a general interest newspaper column for Gannett Media.

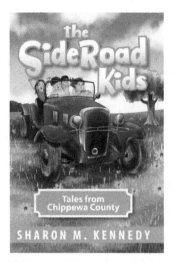

The SideRoad Kids follows a group of boys and girls as they enter the sixth grade in a small town in Michigan's Upper Peninsula during 1957 - 58. This meandering collection of loosely-connected short stories is often humorous, poignant, and sometimes mysterious. Laugh as the kids argue over Halloween treats handed out in Brimley. Recall Dorothy's Hamburgers in Sault Ste. Marie. Follow a Sugar Island snowshoe trail as the kids look for Christmas trees. Wonder what strange blue smoke at Dollar Settlement signifies. Discover the magic hidden in April snowflakes. Although told by the kids, adults will remember their own childhood as they read about Flint, Candy, Squeaky, Katie, and their friends.

"Katie, Blew, Squeaky, and Daisy grew up on farms instead of high rises and used their imagination instead of fancy gadgets to make their own fun. An entertaining read for youngsters. And parents, you might enjoy a nostalgic flashback as well. I know I did."
—Allia Zobel-Nolan, author of *Cat Confessions*

"The stories in *The SideRoad Kids* are often humorous. However, underlying them is a sensitive awareness that being a kid, rural or urban, then or now, is not easy. This is an enjoyable read that will enlighten today's kids about the past and rekindle memories for older readers."   —Jon C. Stott, author of *Paul Bunyan in Michigan*

"Sharon's stories capture the essence of childhood and growing up in a small community. The antics of *The SideRoad Kids* will keep you entertained and take you back to a simpler time."
—Renee Glass, Senior Production Artist, *Mackinac Journal*

"Sharon Kennedy is an amazing writer who draws you into the lives of her characters and keeps everything relatable. She makes you laugh, makes you think, and makes you want to keep reading. *The SideRoad Kids* is an entertaining book about a group of children growing up in Northern Michigan."
—Kortny Hahn, Senior Staff Writer, *Cheboygan Daily Tribune*

From Modern History Press

Printed in the USA
CPSIA information can be obtained
at www.ICGtesting.com
JSHW011042071123
51498JS00008B/6

9 781615 996926